other twisted cedars mysteries

families of twisted cedars

The Lachlans

Katie: Married Ed Lachlan and had two children, Dougal and Jamie. After her divorce she supported her kids by working as a cleaning woman with her partner and friend, Stella Ward. At the age of 55 Katie died of cancer.

Edward (Ed): Former husband of Katie, and father of Dougal and Jamie. Remarried to Crystal Halloway and had daughter, Emma. Killed Crystal during a domestic dispute and served time in Oregon penitentiary. Upon release six months ago, he skipped parole and his official whereabouts is unknown.

Dougal: 34-year-old son of Katie and Ed, brother to Jamie. He played high school football with Wade McKay and Kyle Quinpool. At 18 he moved to New York City and began a career writing true crime novels.

Jamie: 28-year-old daughter of Katie and Ed, sister to Dougal. She is a CPA and works for a local accounting firm. She recently married Kyle Quinpool who has two children from a previous marriage.

* * *

The Hammonds

Jonathan: Former town mayor died two years ago in car crash with his wife. Daughters: Daisy and Charlotte.

Patricia: Jonathan's wife, mother of Daisy and Charlotte. Killed with her husband in a car crash.

Shirley: Jonathan's sister was the local town librarian before she was found hanged to death in the basement of the library when she was 41-years-old. Her death was ruled suicide. Never married, she lived in a cottage in the forest, five miles from town, which came to be known locally as the Librarian Cottage.

Daisy: Daughter of Jonathan and Patricia, Kyle Quinpool's first wife and mother to twins, Cory and Chester. She disappeared shortly after her divorce and hasn't been heard from since.

Charlotte: 28-year-old adopted daughter of Jonathan and Patricia. She works as head librarian in Twisted Cedars.

* * *

The MacKays

Grant: Father to Wade and husband of Allison, he was the Sheriff of Curry County for over thirty years.

Allison: Mother to Wade and wife of Grant. She was a piano teacher until she and her husband retired to Arizona.

Wade: 34-year-old son of Grant and Allison, he was high school buddies with Dougal Lachlan, Kyle Quinpool, and Daisy Hammond. Worked as deputy in Umatilla County before returning to Twisted Cedars and being elected as Sheriff of Curry County.

* * *

The Quinpools

Jim: Wealthiest man in town. He owns the local real estate business, Quinpool Realty. He and his wife Muriel had one son, Kyle. He and Muriel recently divorced.

Muriel: Wife of Jim and mother to Kyle, she and her husband moved in with Kyle after he divorced his wife, Daisy. Muriel became the twins' primary caregiver. A year ago she divorced Jim and moved away from Twisted Cedars.

Kyle: Son of Jim and Muriel, he works with his father at Quinpool Realty. He had twins, Cory and Chester with his first wife, Daisy, and subsequently married Jamie Lachlan.

Cory: 9-year-old daughter of Kyle and Daisy and twin sister to Chester.

Chester: 9-year-old son of Kyle and Daisy and twin brother to Cory.

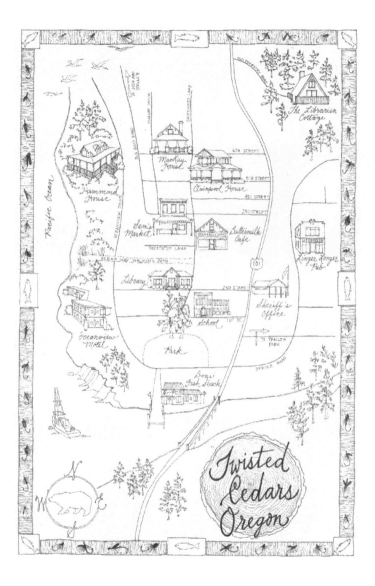

chapter one

july 2010
day of the accident

It was almost noon and Sheriff Wade MacKay was on his way home from fishing on the Rogue River in Oregon when he found the crashed truck, the body, the unconscious woman.

It wasn't often Wade spent his Friday mornings off duty, but a mental health day was in order after a solid week spent investigating the suspicious death and illegal burial of Daisy Quinpool, nee Hammond. Daisy was a friend from his high school days. Seven years ago, when she left her twin children and ex-husband behind, everyone assumed her well-documented mental illness—which began after the birth of her children—was at fault. Regular withdrawals from her bank account had fed the assumption she'd moved to Sacramento, where she was living under the radar.

Not until Daisy's remains were discovered by local true-crime author— and yet another former high school buddy— Dougal Lachlan, had anyone suspected foul play. Making the situation even more terrible, a third high school buddy of Wade's, Daisy's ex-husband Kyle Quinpool, was the prime suspect for the crime.

Law enforcement in Curry County had to deal with their share of domestic violence. But homicides—especially murder—were fortunately very rare. Wade hoped not to see another one for a long time.

In the back of his SUV, Wade had an ice chest packed with the three summer steelhead trout he'd caught. They would make excellent eating, but he wasn't looking forward to getting home, or to the weekend ahead in which he'd focus on the investigation of Daisy's death, probably leading, eventually to Kyle's arrest.

The evidence, so far, was pretty compelling.

And Wade himself had exchanged heated words with his old friend, during which Kyle had all but admitted his guilt.

Wade felt sickest about Kyle and Daisy's two kids. Nine-year-old Chester and Cory were away at summer camp right now. Thanks to Wolf Creek Camp they'd missed most of the drama so far, thank God. They'd been dealing with their mother's absence for seven years already. Now they would likely lose their father to the Oregon State Penn.

Not exactly your classic happy childhood.

Which Wade considered himself lucky to have had.

Back in the days when Wade had been young and summers seemed so blissfully long, he'd fished this same spot with his father. Even then, he'd known he wanted a simple life, like his parents. He loved this corner of the Pacific Northwest, where there were more trees than people, roads that might not see a driver for days on end. He'd dreamed of being the Sheriff of Curry County, with a home, a wife and kids, and one day a week to spend in the wilderness that was the essence of this place.

At age thirty-three he'd landed the job. Now, a year older, he still didn't have the wife and family. Frankly, his love life was a mess. On a day like today though, being unencumbered didn't seem so bad.

His fishing spot was off Bear Camp Road, a narrow and crooked traverse over the Klamath Mountains that linked the small Oregon towns of Agness and Galice, carrying on to Twisted Cedars, Wade's home. He patrolled here regularly, knew every curve, viewpoint and pothole. Normally he would have made it home in under an hour.

If it hadn't been for the accident.

He was listening to Chopin's *Nocturne in E Flat Major* when he spotted the overturned four-axle. He slowed and pulled over. Gripping the steering wheel, he took a deep breath, transforming from man enjoying a morning off work, to first responder at the site of a traffic accident.

The music continued, impervious to the tragedy in front of him.

But Wade couldn't hear it now. He was studying the scene, looking for signs of survivors. But all was eerily still.

Wade jerked his SUV to the far edge of the road, leaving room for the paramedics when they arrived. It was obvious they'd need paramedics. The truck, which had crashed through a guardrail, lay, like a beached whale, fifty feet down the embankment, backstopped by a grove of old growth cedar. Wade could hear his heart thumping in his chest as he put on his flashers and called in the accident. Then he stepped out into the hot, heavy July air and tried to find a route down the embankment.

"Hello! Anyone in there?" He picked his way around dogwood and vine maples, sometime grabbing onto the shrubs to keep from sliding down the steep decline.

No voices responded to his call. All he could hear was the buzzing of insects.

Stamped over the scent of pine and dirt and living things was the acrid odor of burnt rubber. Dragonflies looped around him as he continued to scramble and claw his way toward the wreck.

"Can anyone hear me?" he called out, again.

No answer.

He touched a hand to the truck, which had flipped over and lay on its passenger side. The engine was no longer running, but the hood was still warm.

"Sheriff Wade MacKay here. You okay?" Climbing up on the trunk of a dead white pine that had backstopped the truck's decent, he was able to peer inside the driver side window. A big, balding man, in his late fifties, was slumped over his seat belt.

Blood trickled out of his mouth and Wade's gut tightened. Using both hands, he pulled at the door, working against gravity to wrest it open, until finally he could get his shoulder under it, and gain access to the victim.

He checked for breathing and a pulse, but found neither.

Wade had seen a lot of accidental death in his fifteen-year career. He knew how to deal. You didn't look too long. Or think too much.

Averting his gaze from the death scene, he let the door fall shut, the sound crashing through the forest stillness.

Then he circled the wreckage, to see inside the other side of the cab. Most truckers travelled alone. Even hitchhikers were rare these days.

But this guy had company, a woman with long hair, reddish-blonde and stained with fresh blood. She was strapped into the passenger seat, her body limp.

Thanks to the width of the load, there was space between the passenger door and the ground, about two and a half feet. Wade lowered his body to the carpet of wild grasses and wiggled into a position where he could get a better look. Her weight was partly resting on the door, so he couldn't open it. But the glass in the window had pebbled and he was able to reach in, check her neck for a pulse.

She was alive, but still losing blood from her head wound.

He ran back to his truck for a blanket and first aid kit. He didn't dare move her, but he could make sure she was warm, and staunch the bleeding until help arrived.

When he brushed aside her hair to locate the wound he saw she was pretty and a lot younger than the driver, maybe in her late twenties or early thirties. A diamond glinted on her ear lobe. It seemed to be the only jewelry she was wearing. Her hair smelled pretty, as if she'd recently washed it.

Her jeans and T-shirt looked wrinkled, as if she'd been wearing them a while. But even he could tell they were expensive brands.

What would a woman like this be doing with a burly, middle-aged truck driver? Could she be his daughter?

He called dispatch again, warned them what to expect, all the while keeping a gentle pressure on the wound. Eventually the bleeding stopped. He applied a rudimentary bandage then turned his attention to the miscellaneous items that had fallen to the passenger side of the cab. Anything that hadn't been secured had ended up here, including a black, leather wallet.

Inside was ID for the driver: Chet Walker, age 52, height five-feet, ten-inches, weight two-ten, hometown Klamath Falls. Emergency contact was listed as his wife.

Poor woman would soon be getting a phone call that would change her life.

Methodically Wade examined the rest of the contents. The driver's cell phone, was here, but no purse or cell phone belonging to the female passenger.

The other items in the truck seemed of no significance. Mentally, Wade inventoried them, pausing occasionally to check the woman, and say a few words of reassurance.

An empty disposable coffee cup, a wrapper from a McDonald's burger; a square of pale yellow flannel; a Mariner's baseball cap, foil-wrapped caramels and a package of peppermint gum.

A breeze came up from the west, and a piece of paper wafted up from the cab, floating toward the smashed window. Wade snatched it from the air. It looked like a page ripped out of a book.

Upon closer examination Wade realized it was the Author Bio page from a novel. And the photo staring up at him was of someone he recognized—his old school buddy, now successful true crime writer, Dougal Lachlan. In a phrase that stated *originally from Twisted Cedars, Oregon*, two words had been underlined: *Twisted Cedars*.

What the hell?

Wade had an evidence bag in his pocket. He put the page inside, then turned his thoughts to the woman's missing ID. Maybe she had something in the pocket of her jeans, but he wouldn't be able to get at it until the paramedics arrived.

Wade placed a gentle hand on the injured woman's arm. "Help is coming. You hang tight." Still she gave no response.

Wade mulled over the accident scene. There were no dead animals, the usual cause of single vehicle accidents in the summer when the roads were good.

Maybe Chet had suffered a heart attack or stroke.

Noticing a trail of blood from the woman's forehead to her left eye, Wade used the clean flannel cloth to wipe it away. He wished he could do more. She was awfully pale, terribly still.

"They'll be here soon."

She remained unresponsive. He took note of her left hand, and the pale line of skin where a wedding band might have been. Her nails were painted turquoise.

Wade glanced up at the sky and guessed it was an hour past noon. So much for his peaceful break from mayhem. Then again, he shouldn't complain. At least he hadn't been in the oncoming lane when this truck went off the road.

"Who are you lady?" He spoke again hoping his voice would reassure her, even though she wasn't conscious. "Seems like you were in the wrong place at the wrong time today."

In the distance, he finally heard the sound he'd been waiting for. But even the sirens didn't wake her up.

chapter two

In the summer, the favorite after-hours hangout for the locals of Twisted Cedars was the Linger Longer, mostly because the tourists preferred Wally's Wharf. Wally's had a quaint nautical décor, trendy tapas menu and a pretty rooftop patio overlooking the ocean.

In contrast, the Linger Longer was a no-frills establishment, selling beer, pizza, burgers, and chicken wings. A small dance floor near the front didn't see much action until after ten, while the pool tables in the back were almost always busy.

This Saturday night, Charlotte Hammond, the town's librarian, leaned on the well-worn pine bar while she ordered two draft ales.

"Sorry about your sister, love." Sean Fitzgerald said, while he filled two tall glasses for her.

Dark-haired, charming Sean had been the guy all the girls had a crush on back when Charlotte was in high school. She'd collaborated on a science project with Sean once. She'd done all the legwork, of course. He'd handled the presentation. Even at sixteen he had the confident air of one who'd figured out life and knew how to get what he wanted.

At twenty-eight, Charlotte still couldn't say the same for herself.

"Thanks Sean. Is Mia here tonight?" Sean's wife worked almost as many hours as he did.

"No, she isn't working weekends anymore. Not until we find a new babysitter. We caught the last one making out with her boyfriend on our living room sofa." Sean shook his head, disapprovingly. "Now Mia only works during the hours when her Mom is free to babysit."

It didn't seem that long ago that Sean would have been the boy sneaking in to neck with a babysitter. How had the years gone by so quickly?

Charlotte smiled vaguely, then headed back to her table.

She was expecting Wade any minute. He'd dropped by her house last night to make sure she was okay and to set up the meeting. His consideration was typical of him, and not at all surprising given that, not long ago, she and Wade had been a couple. They'd dated for about six months before he'd foolishly proposed to her on the night of Kyle Quinpool and Jamie Lachlan's wedding.

The wedding had been in May, little more than six weeks ago. And since then, the shit had certainly hit the fan. Poor Jamie must be wishing she'd taken her brother Dougal's advice and called the whole thing off. Charlotte couldn't blame her for her lack of perception, though. Even she, Daisy's younger sister, had been fooled by Kyle. Maybe it was his golden-boy good looks, or his charming smile, but she'd never once suspected him of harming her sister.

Let alone killing her—and burying her body behind the family cottage.

But it sure looked like that was what had happened.

Charlotte took a long drink of her beer, thinking she should have ordered something stronger. She suspected Wade had arranged this meeting so he could bring her up to date with the investigation into Daisy's death. But she wasn't sure she was ready to hear the details.

So far, all she knew were the bare facts. Dougal Lachlan, true crime writer, and very recently, and surprisingly, Charlotte's lover, had been digging up the old garden behind the Librarian Cottage five miles out of town on Old Forestry Road—which he was currently renting—when he'd come across Daisy's remains, wrapped in a large green tarp.

That had been a week ago.

Since then, Charlotte had been living in a state of shock. She'd barely registered Dougal's decision to make his move to Twisted Cedars a permanent one. Last Friday he'd flown back to New York City to pack up his belongings and his cat. She hadn't heard from him since, though it was possible he'd left her a message on her phone.

Charlotte had stopped answering calls on both her home and cell phone. She'd also taken the week off work. So many people, with the kindest of intentions, no doubt, wanted to talk to her about Daisy.

The problem was, Charlotte didn't know much more than anyone else. She had nothing to say.

But she had plenty of questions.

"Charlotte. Sorry I kept you waiting." Wade leaned over to kiss her cheek, before taking the empty seat at their table.

"You aren't late. I was early." It wasn't surprising she hadn't noticed him come in. While it was only eight o'clock, already the pub was hot and noisy. Plus she'd chosen a table tucked in the corner, hoping it would be easier for them to talk.

They could have met somewhere else, of course. But she was grateful he'd chosen the Linger Longer. It might be chaotic and a little uncomfortable. But it was familiar. She felt safe.

Charlotte pushed the extra beer in front of him and was surprised when Wade downed half of it in a few seconds. "Tough day?"

Up close his face was worn down, almost haggard with fatigue. There was a streak of something on his arm that looked like blood.

"What happened?"

Wade's normally bright and observant light brown eyes were dull. He sighed and shook his head. "There was an accident."

Charlotte's stomach muscles clenched as his words triggered a memory. Going to answer a knock at the front door in the darkest hour of the night. Seeing the Sheriff, who'd been Wade's father at the time.

She'd known what was coming, even as he placed a hand on her arm and gently suggested they go inside and sit down.

There was an accident.

Her parents had been killed in a car crash on their way home from the country club.

Charlotte tightened her grip on her glass and took a deep breath. Across the table, Wade was contemplating his half-empty glass

"Anyone we know?"

"No." Wade was quick to reassure her. "Sorry, I should have made that clear from the start."

He was a good man. She was glad there was no residual awkwardness between them. Or at least very little. The reason for that was the same reason she'd refused his proposal.

She wasn't the woman Wade really wanted. His proposal on Jamie Lachlan's wedding day made that quite clear. But while she'd refused him because she knew she was his second choice, her new affair with Dougal made her realize it had been the right decision for her, as well.

"It was a commercial truck, a single-vehicle accident," Wade said. "I was driving back from a fishing trip around noon, on Bear Camp Road, and came upon the scene not long after it happened. The driver crashed down the embankment and overturned his truck."

"It's a bad road." Several infamous tragedies had occurred on Bear Camp Road, one horrifically involving a family on vacation who had been trying to get to the Interstate via what seemed, according to their GPS, to be a shorter route. An early winter snowstorm had stranded them on a side road, and the father perished when he struck out on foot looking for help.

"The driver was dead," Wade continued, "And he had a passenger, a woman. She was unconscious when I found her and still hadn't come to when the ambulance drove off with her."

"The driver's wife?"

"No. Looked about your age, which makes her young enough to be the driver's daughter. But she wasn't that, either.

We've spoken to the driver's wife—she lives in Klamath Falls—and they have no children."

"So, who was she?"

"No idea. She wasn't carrying ID."

"Not even a purse? Or a phone?" Charlotte couldn't fathom walking to the corner market without hers.

"Nope." Wade was clearly troubled by this.

"Did the driver's wife have any ideas?"

"We asked, of course. Had her husband made plans to give someone a lift? Was he in the habit of picking up hitchhikers? She said no to both questions. As far as she knew her husband was traveling his route alone, like usual."

Charlotte could tell from Wade's expression that he hoped for the wife's sake there hadn't been anything sordid about the woman's presence in the truck.

"Besides," he continued, "The woman didn't look like someone who would be hitching a ride. She had diamond studs in her ears. Nails done up nice. Clean clothes—maybe a little wrinkled, is all."

Charlotte fingered the studs in her own ears, a present she'd been given by her parents when she graduated college. "Is she going to be okay?"

"Too soon to tell. She's at the Medical Clinic in Brookings. Last I checked, she was still unconscious." Wade took another swallow of his beer.

His hand was shaking.

This wasn't like Wade. But then, like her, he'd been through a lot the past week.

"We're checking missing person reports in both Oregon and California, too. No matches so far. Hopefully she'll regain consciousness soon and give us the answers we need."

He hesitated. "If she makes it, that is."

"Well. I hope she's okay."

"Yeah." Wade's voice trailed off, then he sighed. "But this isn't what I wanted to talk to you about."

Charlotte's shoulder muscles tightened. She leveled her gaze down at the table. "How did my sister die? Did she suffer?"

"I don't think so. Her head injury was sufficient to knock her out. Whether it was the cause of death we don't know conclusively. I'm expecting more from the medical examiner next week. The final autopsy will be about four weeks after that."

Wade put a hand on her shoulder. "I'm so sorry, Charlotte. I can imagine what a shock this has been for you."

"It's surreal. A part of me feels like I always knew Daisy was dead, and it's good to finally have closure. But another part of me isn't ready to let go of the hope that I might see her again."

Charlotte rubbed her finger in a circle on the table, tracing the condensation from her glass. "I always figured she'd come back to Twisted Cedars to see her children, if not me."

"At least you know she never made the choice to leave. Is that any comfort?"

"In a way. But it's pretty cold comfort when you consider I'll never see her again. We weren't close as kids. Now we'll never have a chance to be close as adults."

Wade said nothing to that. What could he say? Wade wasn't the sort of man to talk, when there wasn't any point. Charlotte had always appreciated that about him.

She appreciated many other things about Wade, too. He was loyal, honorable and kind. The sort of man she knew her parents would have been happy for her to settle down with. She wondered if one day she'd regret turning down his proposal.

"It had to be Kyle who did this, right?"

"He's a strong suspect. First, he was the last person to see Daisy before she supposedly left town. He's also the only one we know who had a grievance against her. We know from her lawyer that she'd been fighting him for partial custody of their kids."

"Could it have been a stranger, Wade? Someone just passing through town, maybe?"

"Hard to understand how a stranger would have been able to bury her body at a cottage only a local from Twisted Cedars would know how to find. Plus, why would Kyle have used her bank card to make it seem she was living in Sacramento, if he didn't have something to hide?"

"That's the most damning thing of all, isn't it?" Years ago her father had set up a joint-account for his daughters. A fund they could dip into if they ever got into a jam.

Ever since Daisy disappeared, monthly withdrawals had been made from random ATMs in Sacramento. While he was alive, their father had kept transferring funds to the account. After his death, Charlotte had continued to do so as well.

Perhaps they'd been foolish to see the withdrawals as proof Daisy was alive.

Maybe if they'd been more assertive with the bank, tried more investigators than the two they'd hired—one when Daisy disappeared, another after their parents' deaths—Kyle's ruse would have been discovered earlier.

"I just wish it could be someone other than Kyle. Not that I'm a fan of the guy. But I hate the idea of my niece and nephew losing both parents. And from all accounts—including Jamie—Kyle is a good father."

"I hear you. We'll have more to go on in a week or two. We've sent some evidence to the lab for testing—hair and fibers found on the tarp that was wrapped around her body. Also blood traces we found on a corner wall in Kyle's kitchen, under a couple layers of paint."

Charlotte frowned. "Blood traces in the kitchen?"

"Evidence suggests she was moved after she died."

"Supposing Kyle wanted to kill her. Why would he do it in his kitchen?"

"We can't assume he intended to commit murder. Perhaps they'd been arguing—they did that a lot, by all accounts. Maybe the fight got physical. A hard shove against the sharp corner of the wall could have been all it took."

Charlotte could feel tears coming, and she swallowed hard. "It's some comfort to think Daisy's death might have been an accident. But if it was why wouldn't' Kyle call 911? Why did he bury her out in the forest—leaving his children, and all the rest of us to worry and wonder what had happened to her?

"It's unconscionable," Wade agreed. He finished his beer, then nodded at her almost empty glass. "Want another?"

"I better go home." Her head had started to ache. Plus she had a feeling Dougal might be returning from his trip today. He'd said he was only going away for a week and it had already been eight days.

She hated to admit how much she longed to see him.

Because counting on Dougal was never a smart move.

chapter three

dougal Lachlan stood in long term parking at the Portland Airport and tried to remember where he'd parked his SUV. Holding a duffel bag in one hand, and a pet carrier with his cat Borden in the other, he needed a third hand to get out his keys.

It was seven in the evening and raining. He'd just spent ten hours flying from New York City to Portland, with a connection in Chicago, and he still had a five and half hour drive to Twisted Cedars.

Home. Strange to be calling it that again after all these years.

But then, a lot was strange these days.

Most notably, finding a buried body in the former garden at Librarian Cottage.

And then that body belonging to Charlotte's sister Daisy.

He was worried about Charlotte. She hadn't answered any of his calls while he was away. Maybe she was pissed at him for taking off so soon after finding Daisy's body. But he had his demons, too.

And he'd had to get his cat.

Borden let out a yowl of displeasure from inside her carrier.

"I hear you." He set down the carrier to get his keys. When he hit the "unlock" button on the fob, lights flashed on a vehicle halfway down the next row, accompanied by a quick beep. There it was.

He tossed his luggage in the trunk, then set up a makeshift litter box behind the driver's seat. On the other floor mat, he put a bowl of water and an open tin of tuna.

It had been a long, confusing day for Borden and she howled at him when he let her out. She ignored the food, sniffed the water, but wouldn't drink it. She did make use of the litter, though.

When he offered her a greenie treat, she wouldn't deign to even look at it.

"Don't think I'm joining you in this stupid hunger strike of yours."

He put her back in the carrier and secured it with the seat belt. Fifteen minutes later he was in the drive-through line for a burger and a soda, after which he filled the tank, and tried phoning Charlotte again.

No answer. Again. Hell, what was going on?

The July days were long, which worked in his favor. He didn't lose the sunlight until he finished the mountain traverse to the coastal highway. Then he had only a few more hours to go. Moonlight was playing on the ocean waves when he finally reached town limits, shortly after midnight. Despite his longing for his new forest home, he drove past the exit to the Librarian Cottage and headed instead to the Hammond's beautiful beach home, where Charlotte lived alone.

The house was much too big for one person. He suspected Charlotte had hung onto it, after her parents' deaths, in the hopes that one day her sister would return. The two story clapboard would have had plenty of space for Charlotte and Daisy, as well as Daisy's two children.

But that was not to be.

A pale light shone from the main floor, suggesting not only was Charlotte still awake, but she hadn't even gone up to her room, yet. Dougal scooped Borden from her carrier. "I want you to make a good first impression, okay? So be friendly."

He jogged up the steps and followed the wraparound porch to the kitchen door, which he tapped on lightly, before trying the door. Unlocked, as usual. For a woman plagued with numerous irrational fears and anxieties, Charlotte was surprisingly casual about practical matters of safety.

"Charlotte? It's me. Are you up?" The familiar smell of her house made him feel like he was truly home. In his arms,

Borden was wiggling so much, he had to set her free. But as soon as the feline's paws landed on the unfamiliar tile floor, she froze.

"Yeah, it's another strange place. But I promise, you'll like this one."

"Dougal?"

He heard Charlotte's sleepy voice a second before she rounded the corner. She was wearing a long T-shirt, her shapely legs and feet bare. The blanket she usually kept on the sofa was wrapped around her shoulders.

Clearly he'd awakened her. "I'm sorry. I saw the light and assumed you'd be up."

"Dougal." She dropped the blanket and ran into his arms.

He hugged her close and for a few seconds couldn't speak. It was such a relief to see she was okay with him. To feel her body next to his, warm and welcoming.

Gently he brushed his hand over her head, smoothing her hair. "I'm not used to worrying about people. Why didn't you answer any of my calls?"

"It's been a rough week. So many people were phoning with condolences and everyone wanted details of what happened. I couldn't deal. So I turned off my phone."

"I called the library. They said you weren't at work, either?" He leaned back to study her face and his heart ached at the sorrow he saw in her eyes.

He'd felt the same when his mother died a year ago. But he'd been too stupid to admit his grief, instead had tried—and failed—to carry on living as if nothing had changed.

"I wouldn't have been able to concentrate at work. Plus I couldn't face the people there, either." Charlotte eased out of his arms. "Was that Borden I saw a minute ago?"

Dougal took a quick look around the room. "She must be exploring your place. I hope that's okay. I'd better go get her litter box and her food and water bowls."

"I'll pour us a drink while you do that."

He could hear amusement in her voice. Up to now, she hadn't seen much of his nurturing side. But hey. If you owned a pet, you had to look after it.

* * *

A few minutes later, all three of them were cuddled on the sofa, Charlotte and Dougal on the cushions, Borden perched on the back. The old cat was cautious, but she'd allowed Charlotte to scratch her behind the ears and under her red leather collar. Charlotte decided they were going to get along just fine.

"Revisiting Jane Austen, are you?" Dougal was looking at the stack of novels on her coffee table.

"My go-to books in times of stress," she confessed. She'd started with *Emma* and was now a quarter way through *Sense and Sensibility*. "Austen is so comforting. As her *Emma* says, *If things are going untowardly one month, they are sure to mend the next.*"

"Pretty quote. I prefer scotch myself."

"Well, I did have a beer tonight, as well. I met Wade at the Linger Longer earlier this evening."

"Rekindling the old flame?"

She checked his expression. When she saw he was teasing, she mock-punched his arm. "No. He was bringing me up to date on the investigation in Daisy's death. Yesterday I handed over the banking records from our joint account. They're going to see if they can match all the withdrawals to Kyle's so-called business trips."

"Sooner they arrest that guy, the happier I'll be."

"It would be nice to have some closure before I plan the memorial service for Daisy."

Dougal brushed his hand down the side of her cheek. His touch gave her delicious shivers, making her feel cared-for and aroused, all at the same time.

"Do you regret letting me rent the Librarian Cottage? If I hadn't dug up the old garden, Daisy's body would probably never have been discovered, and you could have at least had hope."

"But if Kyle did this, he ought to pay. Besides, what good is false hope? The truth is better, even if it's painful to face. Think about Chester and Cory. It's awful that their mother is dead. But at least they know she didn't desert them."

"Yeah. I'm glad for my sister's sake, too. When I warned Jamie not to marry Kyle, I had no idea he'd done anything this evil. I just thought he was a jerk."

"I'm still having trouble believing he did this. Maybe I could picture him accidently getting too rough with her. But burying her out in the forest? Rather than taking responsibility for his actions?"

"Kyle has always been a master at getting away with things. At school he was rich, good-looking, and the best athlete on the football team. Did he take advantage of that? He sure as hell did."

"But think of what will happen if he goes to prison. Chester and Cory will practically be orphans."

"Yeah. It'll be tough on the kids all right."

Charlotte sank her head against his chest. "This is depressing. Tell me about New York. Were you able to sublet your apartment?"

"Actually, subletting the apartment was the least of my worries."

"Oh?"

"It's kind of mind-blowing. Maybe we should wait until tomorrow. It's late and you look beat."

"You can't be serious. I'll never sleep now that you've made me so curious. What happened?"

"You know that neighbor who was looking after Borden while I was away?"

"You said it was an old guy. Monty, right?"

"Yeah. Monty Monroe, or so he said. I thought he was a lonely guy willing to do me a favor by pet sitting Borden. But his motivations were much more devious than that. He was the one sending me those emails. My neighbor was none other than Librarianmomma."

The reason Dougal had come back to Twisted Cedars last month—first time since he'd left after high school graduation—was to follow up on a lead for a potential new crime story about a man who'd murdered four librarians back in the seventies.

Dougal had been tipped off about the series of homicides by anonymous emails—and all his evidence to date had supported the information he'd been given.

Four librarians had been murdered, one a year, until 1974, when Charlotte's Aunt Shirley—also a librarian—had hung herself in the Twisted Cedars Library. Dougal was planning to write a book about the murders, and Charlotte was helping him with the research.

"No! You actually found Librarianmomma? Was he just playing a game with you?"

"It wasn't a game. He was deadly serious. And Monty Monroe was just an alias." From his pocket Dougal pulled out the note Monty had left him in Borden's cat carrier.

Well done, son. Now write the book.

Charlotte read the note twice, then frowned. "He calls you son. Some men, do that, don't they? Even when there's no relation."

"Some men do. But in this case, I'm afraid it's true. I'm almost positive Monty is my biological father, Edward Lachlan."

"No, that's not possible." She studied his face. Realized he was serious. Less than a year ago, Ed Lachlan had been released from the Oregon penitentiary, where he'd served time for killing his second wife, Crystal Halloway. Fortunately he hadn't harmed their eight-year-old daughter who'd been on a sleepover at the time.

"Your father should still be on parole, right? So how could he have ended up in New York City? Let alone afforded to rent an apartment. It's got to be expensive, right?"

"I'm guessing he skipped parole soon after his release and got himself set up with a new identity. I'm also guessing he has money stashed somewhere. God knows how or where he got it."

Dougal rubbed a hand over his face. He looked so tired. But worse, deep in his eyes, she could see pure misery. Dougal hated his father with a passion.

"Are you sure Monty is your father? How is it you never recognized him?"

"I hadn't seen him since I was six. Plus, he'd gone gray and grown a beard, and was all stooped over. Going up stairs he'd complain about his arthritis. He's only in his sixties, but prison must have been hard on him. He looks much older."

"So what happened when you saw him? What did you say to him?"

Dougal shook his head. "Monty—I mean Ed—had cleared out by the time I got there. He left Borden with lots of food, water and litter, at least."

"Did you call the police?"

"Yeah, but they weren't impressed. I have no proof Monty Monroe was really Ed Lachlan. By now he's probably changed his identity again. They'll never find him."

"I'd have no idea how to change my identity."

"That's because you're honest. My dad would have the right connections."

"Did you ever meet his second wife, the one he killed?"

"Absolutely not. My mother cut off ties completely from our father after he left. And her friends, the Wards, made it pretty clear that if he ever tried to contact us again, they'd make big trouble. It was only after I turned eighteen and left Oregon that Ed dared to get in touch with me."

"I wonder where he is now?"

"Far away, I hope. South America would be nice." But even as he said this, Dougal scanned the room anxiously, and Charlotte realized how much this was going to haunt him. From this point forward, Dougal would always be on the lookout for his outlaw father.

And then something else occurred to her. Less than two weeks ago they'd figured out her aunt Shirley had given up a child for adoption when she was sixteen. This child, they'd reasoned, could be the person sending the e-mails, the infamous *Librarianmomma*.

"Does this mean your father—Ed Lachlan—was the baby my aunt Shirley gave up for adoption?"

"Talk about twisted, huh? Good thing you're adopted."

She wrinkled her nose. The alternative didn't bear thinking about. "Why do you think he hid behind that Librarianmomma ID for so long?"

"I would have deleted the messages, unread, if I knew they were from him. I guess he figured if he could hook me with his story, I would get sucked in. And I did."

"Is there any chance he didn't murder those librarians?"

"No. He's the killer. Nothing else makes sense," Dougal said, his voice dead of emotion.

She reached for his shaking hand and held it tight. Pain practically radiated off his skin. It had been hard for him to come back to Twisted Cedars, to the memories he didn't want to face.

Growing up Dougal had lived with his mother and younger sister, Jamie, in a trailer park on the east side of town. His mother cleaned houses for a living, and he and Jamie often had to fend for themselves.

But childhood poverty wasn't what had provided the scars.

Those came from knowing he had a father who was violent enough to kill. Dougal was obsessed with the fact that he shared fifty percent of his DNA with a man capable of murder, and he was terrified of his own dark side.

Charlotte believed he channeled those emotions into his stories for a reason—so he would never turn into the sort of man his father had been.

"Maybe you can do such a good job writing your book your father will end up spending the rest of his life in jail."

"Love the idea. But it would be damn near impossible to build a case after almost forty years. There's no statute of limitations on murder, but I'd bet little, if any, of the evidence will have survived this long. And remember this happened in the seventies. No real ability to do DNA testing, no Internet, hell, crime labs back then were in their infancy. Not nearly as sophisticated as today."

"But still. Isn't he afraid that by confessing to those crimes, he stands a chance of being charged and going back to prison?"

"Law enforcement would have to find him first. And I'm guessing he values notoriety more than his freedom, anyway."

"Sounds like it's also important to him to establish a connection with you."

Dougal's eyes darkened. "And I'll be damned if I let that happen."

chapter four

Jamie Lachlan pulled her car into the Wards' driveway, feeling more lost than ever after a week-long camping trip that had been meant to give her clarity. Instead, she was wet, dirty and despondent.

A four a.m. downpour had caused her to pull up stakes and head back to Twisted Cedars.

But she felt no joy at being here.

The major changes that define a person's life sometimes happen in an instant, like a car accident, or a devastating medical diagnosis. From that point onward, life can be measured in terms of "before" and "after."

Other changes, equally major, take place over a period of time. Days, weeks, months or years.

For Jamie, her change happened in a span of one month and three days, the time between marrying Kyle Quinpool and discovering he'd probably killed his first wife.

In her "before" life Jamie had been a happy, well-educated woman with a good career as an accountant and a handsome, successful husband who loved her very much. Two step-children were part of the package, nine-year-old twins from Kyle's first marriage to Daisy Hammond. Also part of the deal was a beautiful two-story Victorian, about ten times larger than the park model trailer where Jamie had grown up.

Very soon after her marriage, however, Jamie had begun to sense Kyle wasn't the man she'd thought he was. When her brother discovered Daisy's body buried behind the Librarian Cottage about five miles from town—and she herself had found proof that Kyle had been making withdrawals from his ex-wife's bank account to create the illusion she was still alive—that hunch had become fact.

Jamie grabbed her backpack from the passenger seat, then went to the front door. Before she had the chance to knock, Stella was there.

Sixty-four-year-old Stella had been Jamie's mother's best friend, as well as business partner. For thirty-five years they'd cleaned houses together. And socialized, as well. Stella and her husband, Amos, had been like surrogate grandparents to Jamie and Dougal.

And that certainly hadn't changed after Jamie's mom died of cancer.

"I got rained out last night," Jamie said. "And I didn't know where to go."

"I'm glad you came home."

Stella gave her a warm hug, not seeming to mind that Jamie was damp and smelly.

After Jamie had showered and changed into dry clothes, she offered to cook a late breakfast of pancakes and scrambled eggs.

"That sounds delicious," Stella said.

"Is Amos here?"

"Oh, he's been gone since dawn. Fishing."

Jamie hesitated, noting something off in Stella's tone. Were there problems between her and Amos? Jamie hoped not. Their home was one of the few stable things in her life.

Puttering around Stella's familiar kitchen helped Jamie feel normal again. She mixed up the pancake batter quickly, then put a frying pan and the griddle on the stove to heat.

When Stella tentatively asked how she was her anger and confusion came rushing back.

"It's so awful what he did. I just wish I hadn't sold my trailer. Or been gullible enough to quit my job for him. I hate not having a job to go to on Monday morning." Her nerves tensed every time she thought about how Kyle had manipulated her into leaving her job...telling her his accountant had retired and he desperately needed help.

But when Jamie checked with his former accountant, she'd found Kyle had let her go.

Another lie. This one not as serious as the ones about Daisy. But still.

"If you ask Colin Howard, I'm sure he'll give you your job back."

"I hope so." She spooned batter onto the griddle, then stopped to fume again. "How could I have been so wrong about him?"

"You aren't the first woman to be charmed by a bad man."

"I guess you're referring to my Mom and her marriage to my father." Jamie knew very little about Ed Lachlan. Her father had been gone before she was born. According to her brother, she was lucky.

Given what had happened subsequently—her father remarrying, then killing his second wife in a domestic dispute, and serving time for manslaughter—Jamie acknowledged Dougal was right.

But she felt an aching sadness about her father, all the same.

"Amos and I blame ourselves for introducing Katie to Ed in the first place," Stella said.

"Mom wouldn't want you to feel guilty. She made her own choice to marry him." And now Jamie had made almost the same mistake as her mother. Only, instead of marrying a violent man who would one day kill his wife, she'd married one who already had.

"I can't believe no one saw anything the night Daisy died." Jamie added butter to the frying pan. "In a small town like this how is that possible?"

"There are more secrets in Twisted Cedars that you might guess." Stella adjusted the wedding rings on her hand, then sighed and got to her feet. "Here, let me get the eggs for you."

"Please sit down and relax. You work hard all week. You deserve a break."

"Ah, you're such a sweetie. So like your mother that way."

"Helping out is the least I can do to thank you. I have no idea where I'd have turned if you hadn't offered me your spare room."

The house she'd shared with Kyle so briefly after their early June wedding had been cordoned off by the police after they found Daisy's remains. Kyle had moved into his father's apartment, while the kids, fortunately, were still at summer camp, blissfully unaware of the ugly drama playing out at home.

"It's a pleasure to have you," Stella insisted, sounding like she meant it.

Jamie put her arms around Stella's plump shoulders and gave her a squeeze. "I can't stay forever, though. And since Liz bought my trailer, I have no idea where I'm going to move."

"Don't be in a rush to leave. You have enough problems to worry about. Like those poor kids. Who's going to tell them about all this?"

Jamie bit her lip. Despite having married Kyle, she had no legal claim to the twins. And that worried her. In the short time she and Kyle had been together, his daughter, in particular, had come to count on her.

Jamie had promised Cory that she would be still be there, a part of the family, when the twins came home from camp. At the time it had seemed an easy promise to make, because though she'd begun to have uneasy suspicions about Kyle, she'd never guessed he was actually behind the so-called "disappearance" of his first wife.

"Today is their last day at camp. Kyle and Charlotte, as well as the Sheriff, are going to pick them up and tell them the news together. "

"Poor things. And where will they live now? Surely not with Kyle, if he's under suspicion for their mother's death?"

"Charlotte's going to take them. She has lots of room in her house and I'm going to help with the move." Jamie wished she could be given custody, at least temporarily, but since she and Kyle had been married for little more than a month, a blood relative had been preferred.

"What about the twins' grandmother?"

Jamie shook her head. "Muriel isn't up to it."

"She did look frail at your wedding," Stella agreed. "And I noticed she left early."

A year ago everyone in town had been shocked when Muriel left her husband of over thirty years, Jim Quinpool, and moved to live with her sister in Portland.

But Kyle's parents must have known what happened. How could they not, when they were living in the house where Daisy had died?

It could very well be that the strain and guilt had driven a wedge in the marriage and led to the divorce.

"What a sorry mess," Stella said.

Jamie had to agree. In her "before" life, she would just be returning from her honeymoon now. Instead, she was alone again, without home or job.

chapter five

there's something I probably should have mentioned last night."

Charlotte snuggled in Dougal's arms. They were both naked, mellow after making love in the late morning sunshine that streamed through the open window. Across the room, Borden sat on a chair, watching them. Charlotte couldn't decide if the cat looked disapproving, or merely bored.

Dougal ran his hand gently up and down her back. "What's that?"

"The twins are coming home from summer camp today." She cleared her throat, then gazed at his face to check his reaction.

"Good thing they weren't home when we found their mother."

"Yes..."

Dougal shifted up on one elbow. "What are you trying to say?"

"With Kyle under suspicion for Daisy's death, and their grandmother out of town and in poor health, the kids need a temporary guardian."

"Don't tell me." Dougal scrambled out of bed and reached for his clothes. "My sister volunteered, right? Jamie hasn't been married to Kyle for even two months, and now she's going to be saddled with his kids? Damn it, I wish that sister of mine would listen to me once in a while."

"No, not Jamie."

Dougal was pulling out his phone, but he paused at her words. Then he frowned. "So, if not Jamie, then...?"

"Me, Dougal. I've agreed to take custody of Chester and Cory. In fact, Wade will be here in thirty minutes. We're supposed to be at Wolf Creek Camp by noon."

* * *

"So how does Dougal feel about you taking custody of Daisy's kids?" Wade asked.

Charlotte turned her gaze to the ocean on the right. The churning waves matched the way her stomach was feeling right now. "I just told him this morning. He was kind of...shocked."

When she agreed to take the kids, she'd known her decision would likely endanger her fledgling relationship with Dougal. He had trouble enough committing to a woman, let alone one raising nine-year-old twins.

"It'll be a big adjustment."

"Yes." They were about forty minutes from Wolf Creek Camp. Most of the drive up, Wade had spent on his phone checking in on the investigation into yesterday's accident, as well as other Sheriff's Office matters, including a call to the hospital to ask about the accident victim, who was still in a coma.

Ten minutes later, Wade turned off the coastal highway and headed east into the mountains. Wolf Creek Camp was only half-an-hour away now. Behind them, Kyle followed in his own vehicle, far enough back that Charlotte couldn't see his face, let alone his expression.

If she was feeling anxious, she could only imagine how much worse it was for him. She gave a small laugh.

"What?" Wade asked.

"I just caught myself feeling sorry for Kyle."

Wade glanced at her sympathetically. "It's a complicated situation."

They were quiet, then, as Wade concentrated on the narrow, winding road. Eventually he took the final turn and ahead of them were the camp buildings, including the main lodge, two bunkhouses, and a barn for the horses.

The camp had been configured around Wolf Creek which ran a lazy "S" through the property. Wade's SUV jostled as he drove over the wooden plank bridge. The parking area ahead of them was almost empty. Wade had

"Do we go in?" Kyle rubbed his palms against the fabric of his pants.

The coward. He hadn't even acknowledged her presence.

"The camp director is going to bring them out," Wade said.

"They haven't been told anything?" Kyle asked.

"No."

There was no cell coverage out here, only a satellite phone to use for emergencies, so it had been possible to shield the children from the outside news for a week. But now it was time for the truth. How were they going to react? Charlotte had brought tissues with her, she had an entire box in her purse which she was clutching like a lifeline.

"What time is it?" she asked Wade, but he never had a chance to answer, because at that moment the main door to the lodge opened and a man in his thirties with short hair and a small, spry body emerged with Chester and Cory.

The twins were tanned and glowing, excited to see their dad. They ran to him for hugs, not seeming to notice either Charlotte or Wade, at first. Meanwhile the camp director came to shake Wade's hand. "Hi, I'm Braham Fielding." He turned to Charlotte. "And you must be the aunt. Nice to meet you. I'm sorry about the circumstances, though." He cast a worried look toward the kids, who were still swarming their father.

"We had the *best* time," Cory said.

"The horses were great," Chester added. "Mine is called Snoopy. Want to come to the barn and see him? I was one of the best riders, even ask Cory, she'll tell you it's true."

"I was a good rider, too. But where's Jamie? She promised she would be here to pick us up." Cory looked around, as if Jamie might be hiding somewhere.

And that was when she saw the other adults. "Aunt Charlotte? What are you doing here?"

"Hi Cory. Hi Chester." She looked for Wade, planning to introduce the children to him, but he'd faded into the background.

Instead, Kyle took charge of the situation. "We have some news, kids. Come on, let's sit on one of these logs."

The children sat on either side of their father, leaving Charlotte to settle on the next log over, by herself. The camp director and Wade were still standing off to the side, Wade positioned so he had a clear view of Kyle and the children.

"Is Jamie okay?"

Kyle's mouth twitched, as if the question annoyed him. "This is about your mother, Cory. We've finally found out what happened. Why she's been gone so many years."

"But we already know that, Daddy, don't we Chester?" Cory turned to her brother for confirmation. "Mommy's dead."

A shocked silence followed. This time, it was Wade who stepped into the void. He told the children who he was, then asked Cory, "How did you know your mother was dead?"

"Chester told me. A long time ago."

Now everyone was looking at the young boy who, just minutes ago, had been excited to tell his father about riding his horse.

"What made you think your mother was dead, Chester?" Wade asked.

"I just knew." Chester glanced at his father, then at the ground. He dug his sneakered foot into the dirt. "Why else would she be gone? Mother's don't just leave their kids."

The twins had been toddlers when Daisy disappeared from their lives. They probably didn't even remember her. It didn't seem so strange to Charlotte that they would have come up with a story to explain her absence in their lives. She herself, had come up with numerous scenarios as a child to explain why her birth mother had been forced to give her up.

"Well, turns out you're right, son," Kyle said, putting an arm around each of his children. "Your Mom is dead. Last week we found the place where she was buried. The police are trying to figure out what happened to her, and until they do, you're going to live with Aunt Charlotte."

Charlotte's heart lurched at the look of horror that suddenly appeared on the twins' faces. She tried to give them a reassuring smile. *I'm not that bad, promise.* But the truth was, she was almost as afraid as they were.

"Why can't we keep living with you and Jamie?" Cory asked.

"It's complicated, honey."

"So? We're not babies." Chester's face was red, tears pooling in his eyes. Still, he jutted his chin out and stared down his father. "Why can't we stay together?"

"Well, for one thing, Jamie and I have separated."

Cory broke down then. "B-but she promised me..."

"I'm sorry, honey." Kyle looked miserable as he put an arm around his daughter. "Jamie's upset with me, but she still cares about you guys. I talked to her yesterday and she said to tell you that she's going to visit you lots at your aunt's place."

"But then you'll be by yourself." Cory looked stricken.

"Just until the police find out the truth about what happened to your Mom."

"Are they going to put you in jail, Dad?" Chester asked, in a grim voice completely at odds with his earlier tone.

"We have to wait and see, son." Kyle angled his body so neither Charlotte nor Wade could see his face.

Charlotte noticed he hadn't offered his children false hope. Nor had either of the twins directly asked their father if he'd hurt their mother.

Either they assumed he must be innocent. Or maybe they were afraid of the answer.

Kyle cleared his throat. "It's going to be okay guys. You'll see. We'll have lunch with your Aunt Charlotte when we get back to Twisted Cedars. Then I'm going to work and Jamie will help you guys pack your suitcases and move over to your aunt's house."

"J-Jamie will be there? Y-you promise?" Cory clutched her father's hand.

"Yes," Kyle said quietly. "Jamie will be there."

"I still don't want to do it," Cory said. Tears were streaming down her cheeks, but when Charlotte tried to pass her a tissue, she pushed it away.

chapter six

day 2 after the accident

Shortly after the woman who'd been in the truck accident regained consciousness, Wade was notified. He got the call while he was drinking coffee on his back deck. He'd been trying to read the *Curry County Reporter*. Though it was delivered on Wednesday, he didn't usually have time to go through it until the weekend.

But he hadn't been able to concentrate. He'd been preoccupied with thoughts of the Quinpool twins and Charlotte. How had they made out their first night together?

Who would have guessed that telling the twins they couldn't live with their father would be harder than delivering the news their mother was dead? But given how young they'd been when Daisy disappeared, he supposed it made sense.

He sure felt badly for Charlotte, though, trying to do the right thing. He was quite certain neither Chester nor Cory would make it easy for her.

The news that the passenger from the truck accident had survived was a spot of brightness in a dark week. He decided to go to the hospital himself, to get her statement. So far his team had been unable to determine a cause for the accident. Hopefully today they'd get their answers.

As he drove south toward Brookings, he had the windows down and his sunglasses on. He was listening to the local country station—his usual musical preference when he wasn't in a nostalgic mood about his childhood.

Despite the reason for the drive, he was enjoying every minute of it. Mostly the highway tunneled through magnificent forests of redwood and fir, but occasionally it veered out for a sweeping view of the Pacific, the rocky shore, the far-off horizon.

He held his breath each time, awed by the beauty.

He still didn't get how his parents could have traded in all of this for the shopping malls and golf courses of Phoenix. But they told him when he was older he'd understand. Maybe. But he doubted it.

In Brookings, Wade headed straight for the Curry Medical Center. The woman at reception nodded when she saw his uniform. "Good morning, Sheriff."

"Good morning." He noticed a photo on her desk of three grade-school-aged children. He'd always thought he'd have a son one day. A daughter, too. He'd teach them both to fish and camp the way his father had taught him.

"I'm looking for the woman from the truck accident."

She gave him the room number, and pointed him in the right direction.

"Thank you." He walked down the corridor, the sound of his boots on the linoleum floor marking his progress. When he came to the right room, he glanced at the spot where the patient's name was usually written.

"Jane Doe." And in brackets, "Birdie."

The door was wide open. A doctor was at the foot of the bed. Her name badge identified her as Jennifer Schrock, Neurologist. She was tall, with a blond ponytail and dark-framed eyeglasses.

"Dr. Schrock."

She nodded at him. "Sheriff."

He took her nod to be an invitation to enter the room. "Birdie" was the only patient in the two-bed room and the dividing curtain had been pulled back so he could see her from the doorway. She was sitting at the side of her bed, looking remarkably fine for someone who'd been unconscious for eighteen hours.

"How are you feeling?" he asked.

"My head hurts."

Moving closer he could see they'd shaved some hair from the back of her head, but she had such a lot of it, that she could cover the spot if she wanted to. Her complexion was pale, which made her large eyes seem very blue in comparison.

He glanced around the room, noticing the absence of the usual hospital room clutter. No flowers, no reading material, no electronic devises of any kind.

"The name on the door, Birdie...is that you?"

After a few seconds of silence, the doctor answered. "Our patient here is having some memory issues. The nurse on duty last night gave her the name. She said it didn't feel right calling her Jane Doe."

"You don't remember who you are?"

"No," the woman said softly.

He turned his gaze back to the neurologist, who was frowning.

"Birdie are you okay if I talk to the Sheriff about your case?"

The other woman indicated she was.

The doctor motioned for him to come closer. "Birdie's made a remarkable recovery. Reflexes, sensory function and balance are all in the normal range. Some memory loss after a prolonged state of unconsciousness is normal, but when this occurs, the memory loss usually relates to events leading up to the trauma. Usually." She added, to emphasize this point.

"Do you remember anything at all?" he asked the woman. *Birdie.* What the hell had inspired a name like that?

"Name of our current President?" Dr. Schrock prompted.

"Barrack Obama," Birdie responded like a polite grade school student.

"Do you know the current date?"

Birdie frowned. "It's July, sometime. 2010."

The doctor looked at him. "Do you have questions you'd like to ask?"

He nodded. "Birdie, do you remember why you were in the truck with Chet Walker on Friday?"

"No."

"Is the name Chet Walker familiar at all?"

"No," she repeated, more softly this time.

"You didn't have a purse or any ID on you. Do you recall if you own a cell phone?"

She looked down at her hands, moving her thumbs as if pressing numbers on a keypad. "Yes. I think so. I remember four numbers: 0808. Could that be part of my phone number?"

"Maybe." She looked so proud of herself, but he wouldn't get far trying to trace a cell phone with only four digits.

He paced to the window and looked outside, not noticing the view, thinking instead of the possible scenarios that would account for her presence in Chet Walker's truck. She could have been a hitchhiker. That was the simplest, most innocent explanation. Possibly she was a sex worker—but it seemed unlikely Chet would have taken her with him on such a long drive.

It was also possible the truck driver had abducted her, gotten rid of her purse, phone, and ID and been driving her into the forest. But then why would she have been seated beside him, without any restraints?

He turned back to the patient, wondering if the right question might prime her memory. "Do you remember anything before the accident? The smallest detail could be very helpful."

"I'm sorry."

As she covered her face with her hands, he saw the flash of a tattoo on the inside of her wrist.

"What's the tat?"

Slowly Birdie lowered her arms, then twisted her left hand so he could see the capital letter O, with a small mark on the top-right: 'O.

"Mean anything to you?" he asked.

Birdie shrugged. "Not really."

"Any other tattoos?"

Birdie looked at Dr. Schrock for the answer.

"No," replied the doctor. "No scars, or other identifying marks that would give us some clue about her identity."

"What happens now?" he asked the doctor.

"We'll keep her another twenty-four hours for observation. After that, we'll have to release her." The doctor hesitated, then sighed. "There's another complication. Birdie has bruises on her body that predate the accident. I don't believe they were caused by a fall, or another type of accident. It looks like someone had been beating her."

Wade's gaze narrowed on the doctor. "You're sure?"

When she nodded, he turned to Birdie. "Do you remember how you got those bruises?"

The patient looked at him helplessly. "I don't remember anything. Where will I go when they let me out of the hospital?"

She'd asked the question of him, not the doctor. "We have a women's shelter in Twisted Cedars, about a thirty minute drive from here. I'm sure they would take you until we find out who you are and where your home is."

Dr. Schrock gave a small nod, then touched a hand to Birdie's shoulder. "There's a good chance your memory will start to return soon. Not everything, all at once, it doesn't work that way. But bit by bit, you should start remembering."

Birdie nodded, but continued to frown.

"When you're ready to leave, someone from Heartland Shelter will come to get you," Wade said, feeling sorry for her.

"Good." The doctor patted Birdie's hand. "I have to go now, but I'll be back later to check on you."

"Thank you."

Wade and the doctor walked to the nursing station before speaking. Dr. Schrock placed her clipboard on the counter. "I've never seen such a severe case of amnesia, Sheriff. Poor woman. I'm glad you suggested taking her to

Heartland. She needs someplace safe to stay while she recovers."

"Could she be faking it?"

"I doubt it. In fact, I wouldn't be surprised if she was already in a state of distress before the accident. Judging by the bruises, she'd been roughed up more than once in the weeks leading up to the accident." She removed her glasses, placing them in the pocket of her lab coat. "Did you notice the pale line on her ring finger?"

"Looks like she recently removed a ring, possibly a wedding ring."

"Exactly."

Neither of them needed to add the most likely source of the beatings. They'd both seen scenarios like this too often.

On the drive back to Twisted Cedars, Wade mulled over the situation. It was an unholy mess. Marital discord might explain the beatings. But he still had no idea why his Jane Doe had been in Walker's truck. Or what had caused Walker to veer off the road in broad daylight during perfect driving conditions.

chapter seven

Sunday afternoon Charlotte was on the verge of panic, when she thought of the photo albums. Chester and Cory had been playing video games with their hand-held game consoles for hours. Ever since Jamie left, actually.

Jamie had been a godsend. Not only had she helped the twins pack and move, she'd also stayed the night at Charlotte's, calling it a sleep-over and making the night fun for the kids. All four of them had spread sleeping bags in the family room and watched Toy Story 1 and 2 while snacking on popcorn and chocolate milk.

In the morning Jamie had made pancakes and scrambled eggs for breakfast, listened to all Chester and Cory's stories from camp and taken them out to toss a football on the beach for an hour.

And then she'd left.

"Can't you stay forever?" Charlotte had begged, only half-joking.

"They won't get to know you if I'm always around."

Jamie was right, of course. But Charlotte felt clueless. She was comfortable with preschool children—reading circle at the library was one of her favorite things about her job. But she couldn't offer to read picture books to Chester and Cory.

And then inspiration struck. "Would you guys like to see pictures of your mother when she was a little girl?"

They both shut off their games within seconds.

"You really have pictures of her?" Cory asked, her eyes wide.

"Sure. We were sisters. We grew up together. In this very house."

Fortunately their mother had taken lots of photographs over the years. Their father had shot lots of video, as well, but Charlotte figured today she would start with the albums.

Her mother had kept them in a bookshelf in the study, organized and labelled by date. Charlotte asked the kids to help her carry them to the family room where they'd have more space to spread out.

She started with Daisy's baby pictures. Both kids were instantly fascinated. Cory stared hungrily at a photo of Daisy taking her first steps toward her father. "Who is that guy?"

"He was your Mom's father. Your grandpa. Do you remember him at all?"

"A little."

Charlotte pulled out a more recent photo of her parents. "This is your grandma and grandpa Hammond. They died in a car accident when you guys were seven."

"He used to take us to the beach," Chester said, pointing at her father.

"And she made us cookies."

Charlotte was glad they had a few memories, at least. Her parents had adored spending time with their grandchildren and would gladly have spent more, if Kyle had been less standoffish.

When they opened the second photo album, a six-year-old Daisy appeared holding a crying baby in her lap. Her nose was wrinkled as if something smelt bad. And maybe it had.

"Who's that?" Cory wanted to know.

"That's me. I was three months old when the Hammonds adopted me. Look at your Mom's face. I don't think she was very excited about getting a sister."

Both of the kids laughed, but to Charlotte it still hurt. Sibling rivalry in her and Daisy's case had lasted much too long. Maybe, if they'd had a closer relationship, she would have been able to help her sister more after the twins were born. But Daisy had shut out even Mom at that point.

They went through Christmas photos and family holidays—including the disastrous trip to Disneyland when

Charlotte had refused to have anything to do with the costumed characters that populated the park. They'd frightened her, but Daisy had loved them. There were photos of her with Sleeping Beauty, Tigger and, of course, Minnie Mouse.

Eventually they reached the last album, with photographs of Daisy as a cheerleader, then graduating, and soon after that, as a bride, marrying Kyle. There were a couple photographs of Daisy with her infant twins, and in these the transformation from the golden-haired, happy bride, to the depressed new mother, was so shocking, even the twins commented on it.

"Why doesn't she look pretty anymore?"

Had anyone ever explained post-partum psychosis to them? If not, maybe it was time.

"Sometimes, after a woman has babies, her hormones go all crazy. It's rare, but it's a terrible sickness. It makes the mother really sleepy and mixed up in her head."

The twins were both staring at her, riveted.

"Did that happen to our Mom?" Chester asked.

"I'm afraid so. It wasn't her fault and it wasn't your fault either. It was just her body, sending her the wrong chemicals. The doctors tried to fix the problem, but they couldn't."

She thought they'd have questions, but they absorbed her explanation in silence, leaving her terrified that she'd told them too much.

Fortunately the doorbell rang.

"That must be the pizza."

"Yay!" Cory ran for the door. "Did you remember to get mine without tomatoes?"

"I did." Charlotte let the kids carry the two pizzas to the kitchen, while she settled the bill. She wouldn't earn any parenting points with meals like this, but at least the kids were happy. As they sat down to eat, she glanced at her watch, wondering if she'd hear from Dougal.

She'd like him to meet the twins. And, she was hoping he'd stay the night, as well.

But even after she'd watched a movie with the kids, and they'd had their showers and brushed their teeth, she still hadn't heard from him.

"Can we sleep on the family room floor, again?" Cory asked, her eyes wide and beseeching.

"Wouldn't you like to try the beds in your new room? They'll be way more comfortable."

Yesterday Charlotte and Jamie had put the twins' belongings away in Daisy's old bedroom. Charlotte had given them the option of separate bedrooms—the big old house had five—but they preferred to stay together. Daisy's old room was certainly big enough. It was almost twice the size of Charlotte's, with two twin beds and a cushioned window seat overlooking the ocean.

Charlotte pulled out her old copy of *The Adventures of Tin Tin* and asked the kids if they wanted her to read to them, or should they all three take turns?

Chester and Cory hadn't been introduced to the thrills of the Tin Tin stories before, and Charlotte was gratified when they begged to keep reading after her thirty minute limit.

Gladly she read for another fifteen minutes, then told them it was lights out.

She hesitated, then said, "Would it be okay if I kissed you good night?"

Cory happily threw her arms around her, but Chester wrinkled his nose. "I'm too old for kisses," he said.

"No one is too old for kisses. If you change your mind, let me know."

She left a night light in the room and another in the hallway, then went downstairs to tidy up the family room and kitchen, playing the evening news quietly in the background while she worked.

About half-an-hour later she heard footsteps racing down the stairs.

It was Chester. "Maybe a hug would be okay."

She gave him a super big hug. "I bet it feels strange sleeping here. But you'll get used to it. I promise."

"Will we ever see our Dad again?"

"You will. You just have to let the grownups sort out a few problems first. Okay?"

With a trembling bottom lip, he nodded.

Charlotte accompanied him back to his bed, tucked him in, and gave him another hug. In the next bed over, Cory was already asleep, clutching her favorite stuffed dog to her chest.

"Let me know if you have trouble falling asleep," she said to Chester. But his eyes were already heavy. They'd been up late last night. And now it was past eleven.

A big, heavy feeling bloomed in Charlotte's heart as she turned back from the doorway to check them one more times.

More than love, it was the recognition that these children needed her. And that from now on, they were going to be her number one priority.

There were going to be changes in her life. Big changes.

No more late night strolls by herself on the beach.

She'd need to arrange childcare so she could go back to work.

And—most difficult of all—no more sleepovers at the Librarian Cottage with Dougal.

At midnight, she checked on the kids again. They were both asleep now, and while she knew she ought to go to bed, too, she didn't feel she'd be able to sleep.

So she took a glass of wine out to the porch and almost spilled it when she spotted Dougal. He was sitting in one of the Adirondack chairs, his bare feet propped on the wooden railing.

"I wondered how much longer it was going to take you to get your ass out here."

She almost laughed, she was so happy to see him. "Why didn't you text me?"

"I didn't want to look desperate." He reached for her hand, gave it a squeeze and kept holding it after she'd settled in the chair next to his.

It was dark now, and quiet, only ocean sounds to keep them company. She offered him a drink from her wineglass. "Want me to go inside and get you your own glass?"

"I'm happy to share." He sat quietly for a while, then asked, "How's it going?"

She told him everything. How wonderful his sister had been and how lost she felt when Jamie left. Then how the photographs and the pizza and then Tin Tin had saved the night in the end.

"So I made it through the day, but I'm still nervous about tomorrow, and the days and weeks and months after that. They're really going to miss their father. And I don't know how to help them deal with that."

"You lost your parents once. And now your sister. You'll be fine." Dougal hesitated, then added in a quiet voice, "That said, I know what it's like to find out your father is a murderer. It's an awful thing."

"We're assuming Kyle killed her. Do you think there's any chance we could be wrong?"

"If he didn't—why did he go to so much effort to make it appear Daisy was still alive? Anyway, in cases like this, it's almost always the husband. Or, in this situation, the ex."

"I know. I just wish, for Cory and Chester's sake, there could be another explanation." She took a drink of her wine, then passed the glass to Dougal. "Oh, I forgot to tell you what happened when we went to the camp to pick up the kids. They already knew their mother was dead."

Dougal's eyebrows shot up. "Someone at camp told them?"

"No. They'd known for years. Chester said it was the only reason a mother would leave her kids—because she was dead. But I wonder if the kids overheard Kyle and his parents talking about Daisy."

Dougal raised his eyebrows. "It's possible, maybe even likely, that in all these years there might have been a slip-up or two."

He passed back the glass and she finished the wine, resisting the urge to go back for the rest of the bottle. "How is Borden liking the Librarian Cottage?"

"She hates it! Won't go near the door or windows. Spends most of her time up in the loft. I guess she feels safe up there, silly thing."

"Did you work on your story today?" she asked.

"If you mean the one about the librarians—no. I'm going to drop it. I'd hate for my father to believe he'd been successful in manipulating me."

"He put a lot of effort into his plan, didn't he? Imagine the patience he must have had to establish himself as your neighbor for several months before starting to send you those emails."

"Yeah. And offering to cat-sit Borden was quite the extra touch. Believe me, my father used to hate cats. But it seems as if he treated Borden okay when she was staying with him."

"If his goal is to ingratiate himself with you, harming your cat would be the wrong way to go about it," she pointed out.

"I hate that he managed to get inside my head, even for a short while. To think of how I followed up on each of the murders, just the way he wanted me to. Now. I just want to forget the bastard."

"He knows you can't resist a puzzle."

"This is one puzzle I have to forget."

"What about the families of all the victims?" Dougal had told her previously he felt an obligation to them, to lay bare the truth and give them closure.

"I do feel badly about that part." He got out of his chair and paced to the other end of the porch. Then he turned to face her, again. "Even if I wrote the book, the cops probably wouldn't be able to lay charges. My father will never pay for the lives he took."

"Is it possible he was innocent?" Charlotte mused. "Maybe his claim to be the murderer was just the excuse he needed to get your interest."

"I wish that could be true. But no. The timeline works too perfectly. The records to your Aunt Shirley's adoption were stolen in 1972. Shortly after that, the murders started. It's safe to assume Ed tried to contact Shirley soon after he found out she was his birth mother. And she must have rejected him in some way, which set him off on his rampage."

It hurt to see how badly this tortured him. Charlotte went to him, wrapping her arms around his waist and resting her face against his shoulder. "You're probably right. Your father did some terrible things. But you're not Ed Lachlan. And you shouldn't feel responsible for his crimes."

"I share DNA with that guy. Charlotte, if you had any sense, you wouldn't have anything to do with me."

"I don't think DNA is to blame. Something must have happened to your father to make him turn out the way he did. We'll probably never know what it was. Maybe you're right not to let him pull your chain anymore. Just forget about him, and focus on your new life here in Twisted Cedars."

She kissed him then, and after a few seconds, she felt his muscles relax. He pulled her close, ravishing her mouth, making her need for him run hot in her blood, turning her reckless and wild. They made love there, on the porch, in the dark, with the ocean as witness.

Later, they went inside to the kitchen where Charlotte poured them both a glass of wine. She wished he could stay the night with her. But until he'd had a chance to meet the children, it wouldn't be right.

When it came time for him to leave, she asked if he would come again, tomorrow. "For dinner. So you can get to know the kids."

He raked his fingers through his hair and grimaced. "About that. I'm no good with kids, Char."

"Hey, I haven't had much experience with children this age, either."

"Yeah, but you're a nice person, a librarian, no less. You'll be a good influence on them."

"And you won't?"

"Do you really need me to answer that for you? You've read my books."

"So?" She shook her head at him. "Even Stephen King has children."

chapter eight

despite having worked for most of the weekend, Wade found his desk buried under files, messages and forms when he showed up Monday morning. His office manager, Marnie Philips, was at her desk juggling all his incoming calls, motioning with her eyes that she needed to speak with him. Everyone in the office was feeling the stress of having two new cases on top of the usual summer madness.

Wade glanced through the messages, prioritizing in his mind the calls and meetings he needed to make before noon. Within a few minutes, Marnie interrupted, splaying her hands with her perfectly manicured nails on his desk.

"You were in on the weekend, again." She said this like it was a crime.

Marnie was in her mid-twenties, but with her big eyes, clear skin, and round-shaped face she looked much younger. This youthful appearance didn't stop her, however, from acting like she was the boss of the place.

"I realize sometimes you are going to need files when I'm not here to pull them for you. But when you're done with them, please just leave them on my desk."

"Don't tell me I messed up your filing system again."

She raised her eyebrows, silently making her point.

He sighed. "Fine."

"Thank you. By the way Dunne and Carter both want to talk to you as soon as possible. Want me to set up some times?"

The deputies were in charge of his two most pressing open investigations. Frank Dunne was handling the investigation into the fatal truck accident, while Duane Carter was in charge of the Hammond-Quinpool homicide. "Tell Dunne to come in around ten. And I'll meet Carter at the Buttermilk Café for lunch."

"Will do."

He was reaching for his pen, about to sign his approval for Carter's expense report, when he sensed Marnie had something else to say. He glanced up. Sure enough, she was still standing there.

"How was the fishing on Friday?"

He frowned at the question. Friday seemed so long ago now. He realized the fish he'd caught were still in the ice chest. By now, the ice would be melted. The fish would have turned. Crap.

"Weather was great and the fish were biting fine. But that truck accident sure took the shine off the day."

"Too bad about the accident. But do you think you could show me that fishing spot sometime? I went out on Saturday and didn't catch a thing."

Marnie fished? That was a revelation. "It's a MacKay family secret. But sure, you bring in a map and I'll show you how to find it. You have to promise not to tell anyone else, though."

He thought he was being magnameous with his offer, but Marnie didn't seem to appreciate that. In fact, she looked a little disappointed.

Wade turned back to his work, and it felt like less than thirty minutes later when Frank Dunne showed up at his door. Wade checked the time on his computer, surprised to see that, yes, it was ten.

"Come in, Frank. How are you doing?"

Frank Dunne was around forty, a large man who moved—and thought—slowly. He wasn't the brightest deputy Wade had working for him, but he always followed through when he was given a job. He dotted every "i" and crossed every "t." And his impressive bulk was handy for intimidating troublemakers in volatile situations.

"Not good. I can't tell what caused that driver to leave the road. We got the report back from vehicle inspection. Nothing wrong, mechanically speaking. As you know, weather and road conditions were excellent, so we can't blame fog. Possibly a deer or moose ran across the road—but we couldn't see any tracks."

"Maybe the autopsy on Chet Walker will give us our answer. I expect we'll have that by the end of the day."

"A heart attack would explain a lot," Frank said. He checked his notes. "I did call the hospital to check on the passenger. She's awake now, being released today. I wanted her to come in and make a statement, but they say she can't remember anything."

"Yeah. I tried to get a statement from her yesterday. The neurologist says she's suffering from amnesia, can't even recall her name."

Frank looked at his papers again. "I guess she won't be much help with this, then, will she?"

"Afraid not. You're going to have to do some digging. Follow Walker's route the day of the accident. See if you can find out where he picked up his passenger."

* * *

At lunch time, Wade left the office for his meeting with Duane Carter. Slipping on his sunglasses, he made his way along Driftwood Lane, squinting in the blazing sunlight and avoiding the swarms of tourists on the sidewalks.

Summer wasn't his favorite time of the year, anymore. When he was a kid he'd loved the time off school. As a teenager, he'd appreciated the influx of bikinied girls on the beach.

But when you were in law enforcement, the tourists who came every July and August seemed to bring more trouble than they were worth. While the merchants of Twisted Cedars appreciated the extra vacation dollars, Wade and his staff had to deal with the noise disturbances, petty theft, and instances of drunk and disorderly conduct. Then there were the weekend warriors who got lost in the mountains, or stranded on their boats.

Since the Buttermilk Café was only a block from the Sheriff's Office, Wade reached his destination quickly. The cream and yellow clapboard bungalow, on the south end of Driftwood Lane, catered to the trendy and tourist crowds.

Pictures of cows—cute artistic renditions—hung on the walls, and the menu featured items like pancakes and scones made from buttermilk. There was even buttermilk available on the beverage list. Wade had tried it once. Tasted like vomit.

But he tried to spread his business around town, and he knew Duane Carter liked this place. So here he was.

Duane was in his early thirties, too, but as far as interests went, Wade and his deputy couldn't be more different. Wade liked hiking in the wilderness, fishing and beer. While Duane was a fitness freak. He and his wife Lisa were always training for a triathlon or marathon, or some such event. And Wade was always getting hit up to be a sponsor.

On the plus side for him, Duane's mind was as fast and efficient as his body. He got work done well. And quickly.

Wade paused at the entrance long enough to see Duane was already seated at a table. He'd ordered them both lattes, Wade was secretly glad to see. He loved lattes, but on principle—because real men should drink their coffee black, or so his father had taught him—never ordered them himself.

"Hey Sheriff. Think I'll have the kale and goat cheese omelet. You?"

"The turkey clubhouse." He didn't need to think. It was the only item on the menu he liked.

"So—" Wade got down to business as soon as their order was placed. "—where do we stand on the Hammond-Quinpool case?"

"I've got the new gal working on the Hammond bank records which were handed over by the sister. She's comparing the dates to the travel invoices we subpoenaed from Quinpool Realty."

"Good." What had first given Kyle away was when his new wife realized that he was lying about his business trips and secretly traveling to Sacramento—which was where Daisy's ATM withdrawals were always made.

If they were able to match the dates of the withdrawals with the dates Kyle had travelled to Sacramento, that would be a pretty convincing piece of circumstantial evidence.

"We also got the autopsy results on Daisy Hammond," Duane continued. "Cause of death was the wound to her head."

Wade nodded. The case would have gotten a lot more complicated had Daisy still been alive when she was buried.

"The Medical Examiner confirmed she had been moved after her death, which is consistent with our theory about her dying at the Quinpool home."

"Okay. No surprises there." But none of it looked good for Kyle. "Any results back from the lab on those hair fibers we found on the tarp?"

"That's going to be another week. Same with the blood sample we took from the wall at the Quinpool house."

"Any ideas on what we should do while we're waiting for those results?"

"An eyewitness account would be nice. I'd like to interview Kyle's parents."

"Agreed. I'd start with the mother, Muriel. She and Jim separated last year. She moved to Portland after that, to live with her sister."

"Okay. I'll see if I can set up something for tomorrow."

Duane was more than capable of handling the interview on his own. But he didn't know the Quinpools the way Wade did. Screw all the work waiting for him at the office. This was more important. "I'll come with you."

Duane's eyebrows went up. "Yeah?"

"If Muriel saw Kyle push Daisy—and is willing to testify as much—we'll have a slam dunk case."

"You think she'll rat out her own son?"

"My guess is the guilt is getting to her. Why else would she leave her son and grandchildren and a marriage of several decades?"

Wade didn't feel good about putting away his old high school friend. But Daisy deserved justice. And that was his job.

* * *

After lunch Wade tried calling Charlotte at the library, but was told she was on leave. He had better luck with her cell phone number.

"Hi Wade, what's up?" She sounded breathless.

"You volunteer at the Heartland Women's Shelter, right?" He could hear sounds of children in the background. And surf. She must be at the beach with Chester and Cory. Until this moment he'd forgotten she'd been approved to take custody of Kyle and Daisy's children. That must be why she was taking time off work.

"Yes. I bring them books every two weeks, and I run their book club, too."

"That's what I thought. Thing is, Charlotte, that woman I told you about—the one who was in the truck accident on Friday—is going to be checking in at Heartland today."

"So she's okay? You said she was still unconscious when they sent her to the hospital."

"She was in a coma for over a day. Good news is she came out of it. Bad news is she can't remember anything. The staff at the hospital have been calling her Birdie, rather than Jane Doe."

"Poor woman."

"Yeah. And it gets more complicated. Birdie had bruises that pre-date the accident. And a tan line on her ring finger suggests she recently removed a ring."

"So you think she's been going through marital difficulties, and her husband may have harmed her?"

"It's a theory. And if we're right, it's possible our truck driver intervened. Or, at the very least, offered her a ride to get out of a tricky situation. Until her memory returns, and possibly even after that, the safest place for Birdie is at the shelter."

"Definitely. But what would you like me to do?"

"I was wondering if you could check on her next time you're there. I'm going to give Terri a call, too. If Birdie's memory begins to return, I'd like to know. We still have no idea why that truck crashed."

His call to Terri Morrison, who ran Heartland, wouldn't be as pleasant as this one. Terri had a perpetual grudge against law enforcement for not doing enough to protect women against the men who abused them.

In some respects Wade sympathized with Terri's stance. But he had to work within the constraints of the law and his budget, something Terri never seemed to understand.

"It's about time I changed out the books at the shelter," Charlotte said. "I could go tonight, provided Jamie will babysit."

"That would be great." A beep signaled another incoming call. "I should go. Thanks again, Charlotte."

Wade took a deep breath to clear his mind and focus on whatever this new call was going to bring. "Sheriff MacKay here."

"It's Tom."

Dr. Tom Olsen was the deputy state medical examiner. Wade had asked him to call personally when he'd finished Chet Walker's autopsy.

"I've just finished my examination," Tom continued. "I'm afraid my findings aren't going to make your job any easier. As far as I could see there was no medical reason for Chet Walker to lose control of his truck. No indication of his having had a seizure or suffered a stroke or heart attack."

"Is that right." Only then did Wade realize how much he'd been hoping for a different sort of report. The death was tragic, no matter what the cause, but if Chet Walker had driven off the road because of a serious heart attack, it might have been easier on his wife to know that.

Plus, Wade wouldn't have had to worry about what *had* caused the accident.

It wasn't unheard of to have an inconclusive report on a traffic fatality. But Birdie's presence in the truck, her amnesia and her pre-accident bruising, complicated matters entirely.

There were just so many possible scenarios. The driver could have abducted Birdie and she caused the accident when she tried to escape. Or Birdie may have been running from someone when the truck driver picked her up and offered to help. Of course the simplest explanation was that Birdie had simply been hitching a ride because she had no money.

It all boiled down to this: he couldn't be sure Birdie would be safe when she got out of the hospital if he didn't know why she'd been riding in that truck with Walker and what had caused that accident.

chapter nine

Jamie reviewed the printout with satisfaction. Everything balanced, each number was reasonable, the whole statement made perfect sense. There were no problems at the accounting firm that couldn't be solved with the patient application of logic—and she loved that.

It was so good to be back at Howard & Mason, in her old office, dealing with familiar clients. She was grateful the partners—Colin Howard and Ben Mason—held no resentment for the way she'd abruptly resigned two weeks ago. It was as if they understood she'd been manipulated by Kyle, without her needing to tell them so.

Her mother had marveled that her sentimental, romantic daughter had wanted to study business in college. But there were two sides to Jamie, and one of them was organized, methodical and rational. That was probably why she hadn't minded growing up living in a trailer, while Dougal had hated it, chafing under the close quarters, too ashamed to ever invite over his friends.

But as long as you pared your possessions to the essential and kept everything where it belonged, living in a trailer was very doable. Jamie had also thrived with the close proximity to her mother, whom she'd adored. Katie wasn't the type to criticize her kids or subject them to lots of rules. Katie had given them only love and approval.

"The world is tough enough. Home should be a happy place."

That had been Katie's philosophy.

And she'd been right. The world *was* tough. Especially when you were poor. That was a fact. From an early age Jamie had resolved that she would get an education and find a steady, secure job. Of course, she'd also dreamed that she'd meet a handsome, charming man and have her happily ever after, too.

At least one of her dreams had worked out.

Her cell phone pinged, signaling a text message. It was from Charlotte Hammond.

ANY CHANCE YOU COULD BABYSIT CHESTER AND CORY TONIGHT SO I CAN VOLUNTEER AT HEARTLAND?

Jamie answered quickly. YES.

She missed the kids almost as much as she missed Kyle, or, more accurately, the man she'd thought Kyle was. Because clearly she hadn't known the real man when she'd said her wedding vows just six weeks ago.

The firm's receptionist, Bonny Barnes, appeared at her open office door. "Jamie, your brother's here. Want me to show him in?"

"Sure. Thanks."

Bonny was a straight-forward woman, who dressed sensibly and kept her hair trimmed short. She was married to the local postmaster and the two of them doted on their golden retriever, Molly.

When she'd heard about Jamie's predicament, she'd shaken her head.

"You should think about a puppy. There are so many needing a home at the shelter right now."

Everyone had their own idea on what would make her happy these days. Jamie supposed she was about to hear Dougal's.

"Hey sis."

She couldn't help but be impressed with the sight her brother made, standing by her open door, scowling.

Dougal would have made a terrific screen actor. He was terrifically handsome, especially when he was brooding, which was often. And there was a darkness, and a knowingness in his eyes that could be chillingly captivating. If he had gone in for acting, though, he would be the villain, not the hero.

"This is a surprise."

"I've come to take you to lunch."

"It's almost two o'clock. I've already eaten."

"Coffee then."

Dougal looked rough—more so than usual. He hadn't shaved for several days and his eyes looked sunken and darkly rimmed.

"You are so lucky the disheveled look is in vogue these days."

"Like I care either way." He brushed his fingers through hair every bit as thick, curly, and dark as her own. "Are you coming, or not?"

She sighed and set aside her working papers. "I suppose I can spare fifteen minutes."

They walked out to Driftwood Lane, crossed the highway and ended up at the Visitor Information Center. As usual the parking lot was filled with vehicles sporting license plates from all over the country and Canada as well.

Dougal led the way beyond the parking lot along the sandy path that led to the beach.

"Last time you met me here you tried to talk me out of marrying Kyle."

Dougal said nothing, just sat on the same large chunk of weathered cedar as last time and looked out to the ocean.

"Obviously, I should have listened to you."

There were no "I told you so's" coming from her brother, at least.

"You think he did it? Killed Daisy and then buried her body?"

Dougal turned to look at her. "Who else?"

She sighed, then picked up a stick to draw lines in the sand. She didn't really have any doubt Kyle was behind his ex-wife's death. Not since she'd discovered he'd been traveling to Sacramento once a month since Daisy's so-called disappearance, using her old bank card to withdraw money from the joint account Daisy had shared with her sister.

"Do you think they'll arrest him?"

"I imagine they're fast-tracking the lab work and their interviews. Who can say if they'll get enough evidence for a conviction, though." He shrugged. "I didn't come to talk about Kyle, actually. Something happened when I was in New York you should know about."

"You weren't gone long. You must have packed quickly." She was glad her brother was leaving the big city and moving home to Twisted Cedars. She only wished he'd done it before their mother died.

"I was motivated to get out of there fast. I had this old man living a few doors down from me—called himself Monty Monroe. He seemed pretty chatty whenever I saw him in the halls or out on the street, but I didn't think much about it. A lot of old people like to talk when they get the chance."

True. But Jamie didn't think her brother was the type lonely old people would tend to gravitate toward. But there was more to this, obviously.

"Before I left for Oregon the first time, he offered to cat-sit for me. But on this last trip I found out the guy had an ulterior motive. He wasn't being neighborly. He was stalking me."

She looked at him, alarmed. "Was he a crazy fan or something?"

"I wish." Dougal looked her squarely in the eyes. "He was our father."

Her heart thudded. Was it true? "But his name. You said it was Monty Monroe."

"I'm pretty sure he assumed the new identity after he broke parole and moved to New York."

"Did you recognize him?" She hadn't been born when her father left, and Dougal had been little, but their mother had photographs. Not many, but a few.

"No. He'd grown a beard and he was old, Jamie, really old. Plus, his body was shriveled with disease. He claimed to be arthritic and I don't think he was faking it. He could hardly walk."

"So how did you figure out he was our father?"

"When I went back to the city to pick up Borden, he'd moved out. Borden was okay, he'd left her with lots of food and water, but he also left behind a note that made it clear who he really was."

"Where is he now?" Her heart raced at the possibility that she might actually be able to see him, the father who had been entirely absent for all of her life. Was he really as bad as everyone said? But there had to be at least a kernel of goodness. After all, their mother had married him.

Just as she had married Kyle.

For as much as Jamie had come to despise Kyle since she'd found out the truth about Daisy, she wouldn't classify him as evil. He'd been a good father to Cory and Chester. He had been loving to her. He wasn't all bad.

So maybe her father wasn't either. Maybe there were extenuating circumstances behind the death of his second wife that none of them knew about.

"I suspect he's set himself up in another city by now, with yet another new identity."

"Why would he go to so much trouble?"

"I wish I knew. He seems desperate for me to write a book that features him as some sort of serial killer of librarians. Maybe he's just old and looking to establish a connection with me. Or maybe he craves the notoriety."

Dougal's shoulders slumped. He looked so damn tired. But it wasn't just a physical weariness, Jamie suspected. This fatigue seemed to go beyond muscles and bones, setting in to his very psyche.

"He's been playing me along for the last few months, Jamie. Sending me e-mails about some murders that occurred a long time ago."

"The librarians?" He'd been investigating the deaths since he came back to Twisted Cedars, with the idea of writing his next true crime novel about the case.

"Yeah. I think it was his way of trying to connect to me, since I would never reply to any of his letters."

It made no sense to feel hurt that the father everyone kept telling her was a monster who had hurt her mother and murdered his second wife had never reached out to her. But feelings weren't always logical, and that was exactly how Jamie did feel. Despite the fact that her father, from all reports, didn't even know of her existence.

"Did he really do it? Kill all those women?"

"God only knows if anything Ed Lachlan says is true. I'm only telling you this now to warn you. In case he approaches you. I know you, Jamie. Given the chance, you would want to meet him and give him the benefit of the doubt."

She didn't have the nerve to argue the point. Just a few months ago she'd asked Wade if he could help her track her father down. Wade had put her off pretty quickly.

"I hope you learned something from what happened with Kyle. There are some pretty bad people in this world. And, unfortunately, our father is one of them." Dougal stood and waited until she'd done the same. Then he took her arm. "If he tries to get in touch, you call me, okay? Don't wait even one minute. Just call."

chapter ten

Since she was eager to spend time with the twins, Jamie had left work early and Charlotte was able to make it to Heartland before five o'clock. Terri Morrison, a tall, energetic woman in her late forties, with short, brown hair, and expressive brown eyes, was happy to see her.

"Charlotte, I'm loving *Unbroken*, I'm so glad you suggested it for our Book Club. But I wasn't expecting you back so soon."

"I brought some new books." Charlotte set the carton on a chair. "Plus, I was wondering if you had someone new register today? The Sheriff was telling me about a woman who was injured in a truck accident on Friday."

"Birdie. Yes, I picked her up from the hospital today. A real sad case. Poor woman doesn't remember anything. Not her name, or where she lives, or...anything. It's like something from a book."

"Do you think I could meet her? The Sheriff thought it might be a good idea if someone showed her around town. It might help her get her bearings and maybe some of her memories, as well."

"That's an excellent idea. She's been very listless since she arrived. Leave those books, I'll take care of them later. We have Birdie in one of our east wing rooms."

Birdie wasn't in her room, though. She was in the communal kitchen, sitting at the table and watching several of the other women prepare dinner, while four children played around her. A little girl, about four, was coloring pictures at the table across from Birdie, while the other three, toddlers, kept busy with a bucket of toys on the floor.

"Hello everyone," Terri said. "Birdie I'd like you to meet Charlotte Hammond, our local librarian. Charlotte runs a book club for us here and keeps a selection of books for us in our mobile library in the computer room."

Charlotte was struck by an aura of deep sadness around Birdie. Despite bruising under her eyes, and her sickly pallor, she was strikingly beautiful, her features putting Charlotte in mind of the actress Amy Adams. Her reddish-blonde hair was so thick you could hardly see the white bandages protecting her injury.

She looked on the verge of collapse, yet she stood and offered her hand. "It's nice to meet you, Charlotte."

"I'm sorry about your accident. I hope you recover quickly."

Birdie gave a small smile, then glanced out the window. "It's sunny outside, but I feel like I'm walking around in a thick fog."

"Are you in pain?"

"I just took my meds an hour ago, so I'm pretty good right now."

Terri stepped forward then. "Birdie, if you're up to it, Charlotte has offered to give you a bit of a tour of Twisted Cedars. It might help orient you."

"That sounds nice," Birdie said softly.

Since she didn't look that strong, Charlotte decided the tour would have to be by car. "How about I drive you to the main street and we check that out?"

"I'd really like that."

Terri accompanied them to the front street where Charlotte had parked her pride and joy—her father's red '97 BMW.

"It's been a hot July so far, hasn't it?" Terri commented.

Charlotte agreed. "We've been using the air conditioning a lot at the library the past few weeks. Last year we only needed it a few days all summer."

"Today didn't seem all that warm to me," Birdie said.

"Maybe you're not used to the weather here on the coast," Terri replied.

Birdie just shrugged, obviously incapable of confirming one way or the other.

Once alone in the car with Birdie, Charlotte talked about the benefits of belonging to the library. "When you're feeling stronger, I'd love if you came to visit. I could issue you a special library card you could use until—until you remember your name."

"That would be nice."

Birdie spoke so quietly Charlotte had to strain to hear her. She sat very still and watchful as Charlotte drove toward the heart of the town, pointing out the high school and the local rec center on the way.

As they neared the center of town, traffic grew heavier and parking spaces harder to find. Fortunately just as they were approaching the center of Driftwood Lane, a big SUV pulled out, leaving a nice large parking space for Charlotte's coupe. Once she'd maneuvered into the slot, she turned to her passenger. "Are you up to a short walk?"

"I think so." Out on the street, however, Birdie paused, confused amid the steady stream of tourists and locals on the hunt for a place to have dinner. "What's the name of this town again?"

"Twisted Cedars." Charlotte pointed to the small green space where the two famous cedar trees grew, entwined as if they were one. "Locals sometimes say *I'll meet you at the cedars*. This is where they mean. This street is called Driftwood Lane, and you'll find most everything here, from a grocery store to the post office."

Though, what would Birdie do with a post office? Who would she mail a letter to?

"Pretty town. Small, though."

"Yes, but we're the county seat." Charlotte hesitated. "The fact that you say that makes me think you must be from a larger center—a city, perhaps."

"Yes," she said automatically, then stopped abruptly. "I answered without thinking. But it's probably true, right? If it came out so naturally?"

"You'd think so." Maybe she should keep doing this, firing out random questions when Birdie's conscious mind was preoccupied on something else.

They had only started walking along the sidewalk when Birdie paused and frowned. "Do you hear that? A sort of roaring sound?"

Charlotte focused for a few moments. "Do you mean the ocean?"

"Yes, of course." Birdie clasped her hands to her head and smiled ruefully. "I thought it was coming from here."

Charlotte smiled, too. "We can be pretty sure you don't live on the coast now."

"Unfortunately, a city, somewhere inland, doesn't exactly narrow down the search much, does it?"

Charlotte touched Birdie's arm sympathetically. How bizarre it must be to have your memories—your essential self—stripped away in one tragic moment.

"See that path?" Charlotte pointed out a paving stone walkway on the west side of the street. "That's called *Ocean Way* and for good reason. It will lead you right to the beach."

But Birdie showed no inclination to explore in that direction. She seemed more interested in checking out the shops. They strolled a little further, until Birdie paused again, this time in front of Skin Deep, a hair salon and spa that Charlotte patronized.

"I've been getting my hair cut here since I was a little girl." With the sun at their backs, Charlotte could see her and Birdie's reflections more clearly than the row of chairs contained within.

"I think I used to work in a hair salon," Birdie said abruptly. Then she went inside.

* * *

"Do you want a haircut?" Charlotte asked. The surgical team had done a decent job of camouflaging Birdie's injury. But maybe she was self-conscious about the bald spot.

"Ever since I woke up in the hospital, I've felt so weird and useless. Plus, I have nothing. No possessions, no phone, no purse. I need a way to start earning money and I need to keep busy. So I'm going to ask for a job."

Business was at a lull in the store, so Charlotte asked the owner Belle Taylor, if she had a few minutes. Belle was in her sixties, thin, fine-boned and well-groomed. Belle had a big heart as well as a big personality. As soon as Charlotte introduced Birdie and explained the situation, the salon owner gave Birdie a gentle hug.

"You sweet, little thing, you've sure been through a terrible time. If you really have experience, I'd love to hire you part-time. We're overrun in the summer. Plus all my girls want to be taking holidays. But do you have your license."

Birdie held out her palms helplessly. "I don't know. I must, though. This place feels so familiar."

Birdie went to one of the empty chairs, and looked in the mirror. "I've been here before. Some place similar to here, I mean."

On impulse, Charlotte sat in the chair.

Gently Birdie released Charlotte's ponytail, then ran her fingers through the blonde strands. "Your hair is thick and healthy. But it could stand a trim. I'd like to add some layers, too."

Charlotte looked triumphantly at Belle. "Sounds like she knows what she's doing."

"I'm sure she does. Unfortunately I can't hire her in a professional capacity without seeing her credentials." Belle looked truly sorry about this.

"Could I do something else?" Birdie asked, meekly. "Sweep the floors? Wash hair?"

"I suppose we could try a few hours a day, on a casual basis. I wish I could offer more."

They agreed to give the arrangement a try the next day, and set a time when Birdie should come back to the salon.

While they talked, Belle had been eyeing Birdie's hair. "The color of your hair is gorgeous. Mind if I take a closer look?"

"Go ahead."

Belle gingerly fingered a portion of Birdie's hair, then checked her scalp. "You're a natural redhead, with blonde highlights. Whoever did the highlights was a real pro."

Birdie gave her a weak smile. "I wish I could tell you who it was."

Later, as she drove Birdie back to the shelter, Charlotte reflected on the progress they'd made. Birdie was a natural redhead, had probably lived inland, in a city and she'd worked in a beauty salon. It was a good start.

Just before leaving her at the front entrance, Charlotte felt compelled to ask, "Why'd the nurses call you Birdie?"

"It was the older one on duty when I first came in. She said I reminded her of a little bird that had fallen from its nest."

Charlotte had seen them, of course, dazed little things, lying helpless on the ground. The nurse was right. Birdie had that same air about her. She was so still and calm, when by all rights she should be freaking out.

Maybe that stage was yet to come for Birdie. She was probably still in shock. Charlotte had experienced it herself, the emotional buffer that went up after a tragedy. It was like being submerged in the ocean—senses muted and disoriented, everything around you appearing hazy and far away.

* * *

At Charlotte's home, Jamie had made pasta and a salad for dinner. Charlotte arrived at the perfect time to share the meal, but the conversation went on around her, almost as if she wasn't there. If the kids were trying to prove they were closer to their step-mother than to her, then they succeeded.

Charlotte knew it was immature of her to care. The welfare of the children was what mattered, and the fact that they were laughing and chattering—well, Cory was. Chester, as usual, was rather quiet—was all that mattered.

After the meal was over, Jamie helped the kids load the dishwasher, then wipe down the countertops. "I have to go soon, but first we need to talk about our plan."

arranged with the camp director for them to pick up the twins two hours before the other campers' parents were scheduled to arrive.

"I just wish I knew them better," Charlotte said, her gaze fixed on the Lodge where all the children would be gathered for lunch.

"Your wish is about to come true." Wade parked, killed the engine, then turned to her. "Ready?"

She sighed.

At that moment, Kyle pulled in beside them. He was wearing sunglasses, but when he glanced in her direction, Charlotte felt a shiver zing down her spine.

This was the first time she'd seen him since she'd found out about Daisy. Not that she'd seen much of Kyle previously. She'd always sensed he didn't like her, and that was why he made it so difficult for her to spend time with her niece and nephew.

But now it seemed more likely that being around her had reminded him of his guilt.

Charlotte was not a violent person. But when Kyle got out from behind the wheel, dressed as if he'd just come off the golf course, she wanted to pummel him with her fists. It was so unfair, that Kyle should be enjoying his life, when he'd stolen her sister's.

As if sensing her agitated emotional state, Wade took her arm and guided her toward the lodge. "Must be hard for you to be around him. But try to keep your cool. Remember we're here for the children."

Charlotte took a deep breath. Wade was right. She had to remain calm. They walked as far as the outdoor campfire site. It was a gorgeous summer day, with cotton ball clouds in a baby blue sky. The good weather made their mission seem all the more surreal.

Behind her, she could hear Kyle walking through the grass toward them. A moment later he was standing on Wade's other side, his gaze fixed on the main door of the lodge.

"What plan?" Chester sounded immediately suspicious.

Charlotte and Jamie exchanged glances. Earlier Charlotte had asked Jamie for her advice on how to deal with the new reality of having custody of two children. How was she to continue working or have any semblance of a social life?

Together they'd worked out a schedule.

"I know you wish life could go back to the way it was before summer camp," Jamie began. "But it can't. Not for a while, anyway."

"How long?" Chester wanted to know.

"We can't say. All we can do, your Aunt Charlotte and I, is try to make sure things are as okay for you guys as possible. Most importantly, you have to be safe."

"We were safest with Dad," Chester insisted.

"There are laws in this country that are meant to protect children, for those cases where their parents really did commit a dangerous crime."

"But our dad didn't!"

"Yes, but until he has a chance to prove that, this is what we're going to do."

Jamie somehow managed to keep her tone cheerful and authoritative and Charlotte admired her immensely for this.

"Your aunt has to go back to work at the library, so you guys are going to spend your days with Nola Thompson again."

They both groaned and Charlotte felt terribly guilty. Jamie had forewarned her the twins weren't fond of their former babysitting arrangement. But it had sufficed in the years after Kyle's mother moved to Portland, and it would have to suffice again.

At least until Charlotte thought of something more suitable.

"You'll spend most of your evenings and weekends here with your Aunt Charlotte. But I'm going to keep coming over often—at least two or three times a week. How does that sound?"

Both the twins were too polite to complain out loud. But Charlotte could tell by the way they avoided eye contact with her that they'd been hoping for more time with Jamie.

chapter eleven

It had been a long day and Wade was looking forward to a beer and a burger at the Linger Longer, but Duane Carter caught up to him just as he was about to lock his office door. Wade waved the deputy inside, and closed the door behind them.

"Sheriff, we've had a new development." Duane spoke quickly, his eyes sharp, his muscles tense. Momentarily he perched on the edge of a chair, then sprang out of it, and began to pace from the window, back to Wade's desk.

"I wasn't having any luck obtaining Muriel Quinpool's address in Portland, so I called her son and Kyle admitted his mother wasn't living in Portland as everyone thought—but in Sacramento." Carter paused, letting the significance of this sink in.

"The withdrawals from Daisy Hammond's bank account were made from ATMs in Sacramento."

"Yes. We have video footage from several of the more recent withdrawals—all were made by a woman with a large hat, sunglasses and gloves. And that had us puzzled, at first. We thought maybe Kyle was paying someone to make the withdrawals for him."

"But he was using his mother." Wade obligingly drew the obvious conclusion.

"Exactly. It's pretty darn clever, when you think of it. The gloves were a smart touch. Nothing shows the age of a woman better than her hands."

"I wonder who made the withdrawals for him before Muriel left Twisted Cedars?"

"I wondered the same thing. So I went to those reports Charlotte Hammond received from the investigator she hired to find Daisy after their parents died. The P. I. checked the video footage from the ATMs, too. According to his report, a different woman made the withdrawal every time."

"So how did he explain that?"

"He guessed that Daisy was asking friends to make the withdrawals for her, so she wouldn't get caught on camera."

"I bet if Kyle offered a woman on the street a hundred bucks to make the withdrawals for him, not many would have refused."

"Exactly. And most of the withdrawals were made in less affluent, more blue-collar and sometimes even rough areas of the city. Quinpool wouldn't have to ask too many before someone said yes."

Wade nodded. "I agree. But with two years having gone by, I doubt we'd be able to locate any of those women."

"It would be a needle in the haystack job," Carter agreed. "Good thing we have Muriel."

Wade leaned back in his chair, rubbed his chin. "I'll bet Kyle coerced her into making those withdrawals. Hopefully this will help our case when we go to talk to her. The guilt must be crippling for her."

"She doesn't have to know we can't ID her from the video footage. If she thinks we have her nailed for fraud, she might be more inclined to talk about how Daisy died."

"Maybe. Hopefully. Sure would be nice to tie this up with a pretty bow like a confession."

Duane sported a brief grin, then sobered up fast.

From experience, they both knew it wasn't wise to assume you had an investigation in the bag before you actually did. And even when you figured you had all your evidence stacked so neatly a judge or jury would have to commit—a clever lawyer might come up with some way to make that evidence inadmissible.

They had to proceed with caution. And entirely by the book.

"Do you have our travel arrangements made?"

"Yup. I booked an early morning flight from Crescent City. Want me to pick you up around six?"

"I'll drive." Wade got up from his desk, planning to actually make it to the Linger Longer this time. "Care to join me for a beer and burger?"

Duane looked appalled. "Megan's buying some trout and fixings for a salad. Thanks anyway."

Wade frowned. Duane's mention of trout reminded him. He still hadn't emptied out that damn ice chest.

* * *

As Wade exited his office, he noticed Dunne chatting up Marnie, who was in the process of clearing off her desk for the night. Now that he thought about it, he realized he'd seen Dunne hanging around Marnie's work space a lot lately. He sure hoped his deputy realized he was far too old, and out-of-his league, for Marnie.

"Seems like everyone is working late tonight," Wade commented. "I'm off to the pub, myself. Suggest you both call it a day, as well."

The silly smile on Dunne's face vanished and he stood taller. "Yes, Sheriff."

"I was just about to leave," Marnie said. "Would you like some company, Sheriff?"

"Good idea." She probably wanted to give Dunne the slip. Wade put an arm around his deputy's shoulders. "How about you join me for a beer and a bite to eat? I'd like an update on the Walker investigation."

"I guess, Sheriff."

With a regretful look at Marnie, Dunne fell into step beside Wade.

Wade turned back to give Marnie a wink, but she was frowning at him. Had he read the situation incorrectly? Surely Marnie didn't mean to encourage Dunne's attentions?

The pub was a mere ten minute walk away, and once inside, Wade chose the table in the corner, far from the noise of the pool tables in the back.

Dunne was pretty quiet, with a sullen set to his face. He'd given the shortest answers possible to Wade's questions about his vacation plans—he had two weeks booked off in

September. Wade guessed the deputy hadn't been happy to have his conversation with Marnie interrupted.

But that might not be the only reason for his attitude. As one of the more experienced deputies in Curry County, Dunne may have had his eye on the Sheriff position before Wade came home to run for the job. Wade knew his years as deputy in Umatilla County, hadn't counted as much with voters, as his last name. His father had been a popular sheriff.

Wade didn't intend to ride his daddy's coattails, though. He meant to prove he was his own man, and he'd work with Dunne—as long as the man met him halfway.

Dunne kept up the silence until their beers came. He hadn't ordered a burger, which Wade took as a sign that he wanted to keep this encounter as short as possible.

Might as well get down to business. "Did you have any luck tracing Walker's route the day of the accident?"

Dunne shifted forward in his chair. "I started with Walker's wife. Name is Leanne. She sounded pretty choked up. Said her husband was a good driver, with an excellent safety record. She wanted to know why he would have gone off the road like that, and I told her we were wondering the same damn thing."

Wade listened, nodding. No sense asking Dunne to cut to the chase. He was going to walk them through this one step at a time.

"She told me her husband had a perfect bill of health at his last physical. Maybe he ate too much junk food on the road. But at home, she cooked good meals, lots of vegetables."

Before Dunne could pass on more details about Leanne Walker's menu plans, Wade jumped in. "Did you ask her about the passenger?"

"I did, though I felt it was a touchy subject. Leanne said her husband didn't fool around with women and wasn't in the habit of picking up hitchhikers, either. He liked to listen to audio books when he was on the road. Hitchhikers talk too much."

"As far she knew, then, Chet hadn't offered anyone a lift?"

"No. He was just doing one of his regular runs up the coast to Coos Bay. Left his home around eight-thirty Friday morning, went to load up his truck and called his wife when he was on his way about an hour later. She didn't hear anything from him after that."

"Go on."

Dunne pulled his notebook out of his pocket. "I asked his wife to go online and see where he'd made his last purchases. He uses a company credit card when he travels, and she keeps the books for him, so she had no problem doing that."

"Good. And what did she find?"

"He gassed up at the North Valley Shell in Medford," Dunne said. "Must have been shortly before he turned off the Interstate to head through to the coast."

"What time was that?"

"Around noon. He probably had lunch at the same time, judging from the amount of the bill. There were no more credit card purchases after that."

Wade took a long drink of beer. There was definitely something sad about tracking a man's last actions before he died. Where had Chet made the fateful decision to offer a ride to Birdie? And had it been that decision that had led to the accident?

Or would the truck have crashed with or without Birdie in the passenger seat?

They were still a long way from having the answer to those questions.

"Did you check if Chet was caught on video at the gas station?"

"I did. The manager was cooperative and has already emailed me the footage. Chet ate alone, and there was no one in his truck when he drove away from the pumps. So he must have picked up his female passenger somewhere between Medford and the turn off to Bear Camp Road."

"Or, his passenger was slumped down, sleeping or hiding, and wasn't picked up by the camera."

"I hadn't thought of that." He gave Wade a grudging look of respect, before continuing. "Another thing—Leanne said she didn't know why her husband would have taken Bear Camp Road. He usually took the 42."

chapter twelve

Cory had crept into Chester's bed, and had her hand resting on his back, when Charlotte went to their room to check on them late Monday evening. She moved in closer and saw tear tracks down Cory's cheeks. Chester's were dry. Was he tougher? Or just bottling in his fear and sadness?

Charlotte pulled the light blanket up to their shoulders. It was a warm evening, they wouldn't need more. Gently she dropped a kiss on the top of each head. Their hair smelled like ocean water. Jamie must have taken them to the beach while she was touring Birdie around town.

Quietly she withdrew from the room, turning out the hall light, but leaving the two night lights burning. It was almost eleven, she should go to bed herself.

She'd finished reading *Sense and Sensibility* and was looking forward to moving on to her favorite Jane Austen novel.

But the old restlessness was tugging at her. In the past she would escape to the beach, and walk along the edge of the ocean until she felt tired. Tonight, however, she poured herself a glass of wine and went out to the porch. She sat in the dark and wished Dougal would magically appear, like last time.

But he didn't.

She sipped her wine and stared into the darkness. Her emotions tangled like seaweed, reflective of a life which was far more complicated than it had ever been before.

She was ashamed to admit, even to herself, that she felt some resentment for how becoming the twins' guardian was changing her life. Her relationship with Dougal was the most exciting thing that had ever happened to her—and now it was being hobbled by her new, engulfing, commitments.

And there were other changes. Needing to find appropriate childcare so she could continue working. Worrying about providing meals that were nutritious but also appealing to younger palettes. Eventually, when the twins were ready for their own rooms, she'd have to do some re-decorating and furniture shopping. And she was even going to have to buy a new car, since only two could sit comfortably in her coupe.

Those were her selfish concerns, and she hated owning up to them.

But she also felt sorrow—for the way Daisy's life had ended, and for all that had been lost, not only to Daisy, but to those little kids up there. If Daisy had lived, she might well have had a full recovery, and been able to be the mother Chester and Cory deserved.

It was amazing, in a way, that they were as normal as they were. As far as Charlotte knew, their grades were fine, they got on well with most kids at school, and they had a healthy interest in swimming, football and riding their bikes. They were mostly polite, not too messy, and the way they stuck up for one another proved they were loyal and loving.

She supposed Kyle had earned some of the credit for this.

But if he was responsible for Daisy's death—he was going to go to prison, probably for ten years or more. By then the twins would be nineteen.

Charlotte sighed, then pulled out her phone. Dougal had sent a text message an hour ago, but she'd had her phone on mute and had missed it.

EVERYTHING OKAY?

She called him back. "Hey there. I'm out on the porch, wishing you were here."

"I'm wishing the same thing. I started outlining a new book today."

"Tell me about it."

"It's going to be fiction. I'm tired of dealing with reality."

She laughed. "I know the feeling."

"Kids doing okay?"

"They're sad." She pictured them cuddled together in the single bed, like puppies finding comfort from merely being together. "I should check into counselling for them. This situation is so difficult."

"They're caught in the middle."

"Exactly. And now, so am I. For Daisy's sake, I want Kyle to be arrested and serve his time. But when I think of what's best for Daisy's children, I'm pretty confused. Is it even possible to be a good parent and also a murderer?"

"That brings multi-tasking to a new level."

"These are the sort of problems I expect to see on reality TV. Not in my own life." She thought about Birdie. "But I suppose I shouldn't complain. At least I still have most of my marbles. Did you hear about the woman who was in the truck accident on Friday?"

"The one who was in a coma?"

"Yes. She came out of it—but she can't remember anything. Not who she is, or why she was in that truck in the first place."

"Is she still in the hospital?"

"No, she's at the Heartland Women's Shelter. I gave her a tour of our town this evening while Jamie was with the twins."

"Why at the women's shelter? Isn't that just for abused women?"

"It's possible she fits in that category. Wade has a theory that she may have been running from an abusive husband when the truck driver picked her up."

"How did she seem to you?"

"Sad and lost. I think she's still in shock. One of the nurses named her Birdie and it's stuck. Oh, something interesting happened when we walked by Shear Madness. Suddenly Birdie remembered she'd been a hair dresser."

"Did she remember anything else?"

"No. But she went inside and asked Belle Taylor for a job."

"Seriously?"

"She must feel pretty vulnerable. Can you imagine having no money, credit cards or ID?"

"So did Belle give her a job?"

"You know what a big heart Belle has. Without a social security number or credentials, she couldn't hire her as a stylist. But she's giving her a few casual hours, shampooing and sweeping, that sort of thing."

"Interesting."

"Is it?"

"I've never met anyone suffering from amnesia before." After a brief pause he continued. "Weren't you just saying my hair is getting a little long?"

Charlotte shook her head, amused, but not surprised.

Dougal could claim he wanted to try his hand at fiction.

But it was the real life mysteries that got him, every time.

chapter thirteen

day 4 after the accident

muriel Quinpool lived in an upscale condo complex overlooking east Sacramento. Mature oak trees guarded the perimeter, while the inner courtyard was colorful and lush with summer flowers. Wade's mother had been a gardener. He felt sure she would have approved.

"Posh place," Duane commented as they waited to be admitted by the doorman.

The portly man seemed annoyed to lift his head from his newspapers. He told them to take the elevator up to the fourth floor, then bowed over the sports page again.

Of course Duane had to take the stairs. Wade followed, albeit at a slower pace. He supposed the exercise wouldn't hurt.

Muriel took a long time to answer the door, after their knock. Despite the fact that Duane had warned her they'd be coming, she had a puzzled frown as she looked from one of them to the other.

"Hello, Mrs. Quinpool," Wad said. "Sorry to disturb you, but we have a few questions."

"Oh. Yes. Wade. Please come in."

She looked gaunt and tired, much as Wade remembered her from Kyle and Jamie's wedding in May. She was dressed nicely, though, and wore a pearl necklace Wade recalled from when he was a kid. To his memory, he'd never seen her without it.

She inclined her head when he introduced his Deputy Duane Carter, but said nothing else, just indicated they should follow her to the sitting room off the entrance. On the coffee table next to the sofa were two glasses of water, with ice and a slice of lemon. She waved her hand at the sofa and Wade and Carter each took a side.

As for Muriel, she settled in the high back chair facing them, as primly as the Queen of England, with her hands in her lap and her ankles crossed.

"How are you, Mrs. Quinpool?" Wade asked.

"Not in the best health, I'm afraid."

"Oh?" When Child Services was looking to find the appropriate guardian for Chester and Cory, Muriel had demurred because of her health. "Nothing too serious, I hope?"

"Oh, aches and pains, mostly. Trouble sleeping. The normal complaints that come with aging."

During his school years, Wade had spent a fair amount of time at Kyle's house. But Muriel had always been in the background, not the sort of mother to offer a plate of home baked cookies, or try to chat with her son's friends to get to know them.

Back then, her reticence had been appreciated. Wade and his pals had loved having free rein in the Quinpool's basement, and there were always lots of chips and sodas to snack on in the kitchen.

Besides, if they wanted home baked cookies all they had to do was go to Wade's house. Wade felt sad, thinking of those old days now.

"You've heard, no doubt," Duane began taking the lead when Wade was slow to do so, "that Daisy Hammond's body was found buried in the garden at the Hammond's cottage off Old Forestry Road."

She wrinkled her nose in distaste. "Yes. I heard."

Wade glanced at Duane, giving him silent approval to continue.

"Daisy died from a blow to her head, Mrs. Quinpool. Your son, Kyle, told everyone—including Daisy's children, her parents and her sister—that she'd run out on them. But she hadn't. All these years Daisy has been dead. Buried illegally, without benefit of a service or even a coffin."

Partway through Duane's statement of facts, Muriel lowered her gaze to her hands.

She looked very old. Very frail. But Wade couldn't afford to feel sorry for her. The point was to play on her guilt, hopefully building the pressure to a point where she would be ready to unburden herself of the weight.

"For Daisy's sake, but especially for Chester and Cory's sake, the truth needs to be told," Wade added.

"What makes you think I know anything?" Muriel asked, her voice so soft Wade could hardly hear it.

"You and Jim were living with Kyle and the kids at that time," Wade said. "If Kyle and Daisy had a fight when Daisy was visiting—you would have heard it. We found Daisy's blood on the corner wall next to the kitchen counter. Kyle pushed her, didn't he Mrs. Quinpool? I'm sure he never meant to hurt her. It was just terrible luck that her head happened to hit that sharp corner wall."

Muriel was breathing faster now, rubbing the skin on the back of her hands in a compulsive fashion. "I don't think that happened. You're trying to trick me."

"We only want you to tell the truth," Duane said, his tone sharp. "After all, you don't want to perjure yourself."

"Perjure," Muriel repeated, as if she was unsure what it meant.

"Lying to law enforcement officials is a crime," Wade said. "I'm sure you know that."

"B-but I'm not lying. I just don't *know*!" She popped out of her chair as if the pressure of remaining sitting had become too much. She went to an antique bureau where family photos were displayed—including her wedding photo.

Wade joined her, picking up the photo as if it had just caught his eye. "Wow, you and Jim made a handsome couple."

Muriel bit her bottom lip, then gave the slightest of nods.

"It's nice you hung onto this photo." Wade carefully placed it back on the wooden surface.

"Why wouldn't I?"

"Most divorced women pack away their wedding photos, or give them to their children, don't they?"

A red stain crept up Muriel's cheeks. "We had a lot of happy years. I refuse to focus only on the bad."

"What did happen to you and Mr. Quinpool?" Wade asked. "It had to be something pretty serious considering all the years you'd been together, and the full life you had in Twisted Cedars. Not to mention your son and grandchildren."

"That's private. You have no reason to ask about that." Her eyes narrowed and her lips thinned. "You have some nerve Wade MacKay. We welcomed you into our house. You were one of Kyle's best friends."

Wade didn't need her to point any of this out. He was all too aware of the past they had all shared. "We have to ask these questions. Daisy Hammond was my friend, too, Mrs. Quinpool."

"Here's a possible scenario," Duane stepped in, to keep up the pressure. "Let's say your husband is the one who talked your son into covering up the accident and burying Daisy's body."

Duane left the sofa and walked around to Muriel's other side. She must have felt overwhelmed, with two much taller men so close. She tried to step backward but the cabinet was in her way, and she was forced to stay put.

"And let's assume that you, Mrs. Quinpool, were against the plan," Duane continued. "But you didn't want to betray your husband and son so you kept quiet. As the years went by, you probably began to feel more and more guilt. Especially as you had to watch Daisy's children grow up, never suspecting what had really happened to their mother."

Muriel covered her face with her hands, and shook her head. "No! That's not what happened."

"Then what did happen?" Wade pressed gently. "We know Kyle buried her. We're having hairs found at the burial site tested. We'll soon be able to prove that they are his. Why did your son bury Daisy's body? If she died by accident, why not call 911?"

"I can't breathe! I need water."

Wade and Carter exchanged a glance. Wade was positive she'd seen or heard something. Or maybe Jim had, and then had shared his knowledge with his wife.

Muriel was showing classic signs of guilt by association.

But he didn't dare press her too hard.

He took one of the untouched glasses from the table and handed it to her. "Maybe you should sit down."

He and Duane stayed with her for another fifteen minutes. They calmed her down, then asked her the same questions, over and over. She didn't change her story a bit, just kept insisting she didn't know anything.

Next they questioned her about the withdrawals from Daisy's bank account. As planned, Duane insinuated they would be able to identify her from the video footage.

She only increased her denials. Her insistence they were trying to trick her.

Eventually Wade circled back to the night Daisy died.

"How could you have slept through the argument, and all that commotion?" Wade asked. "It just doesn't wash."

"I used to wear ear plugs to bed. Because of Jim's snoring."

Wade went for the opening. "So you admit there was an argument—you just didn't hear it. Did your husband tell you about it the next day?"

"No. No. You're twisting my words. Jim told me nothing. There was nothing to tell."

chapter fourteen

W hat are your plans for the rest of the day?" Charlotte fastened her bra, adjusted her breasts, then put her blouse back on.

God, he loved watching the librarian dress.

Dougal was propped up in her bed, arms crossed behind his head. She'd opened the curtains and the bright noon-hour sunshine pooled on the foot of the bed where she was sitting.

"My plans? Gosh, Charlotte, let me check my day planner."

Even as she laughed, she shook her head. "I couldn't live that way. I need discipline. Order. Routine."

He cringed.

"Will you be here when the kids and I get home around five?"

"I'll probably go back to the cottage to do some writing. But I can come back. If you want me."

"Oh, I do." She leaned over to give him a kiss.

He caught her hand before she moved away. "As long as we're clear I'm not playing the role of surrogate uncle to the twins."

She hesitated, then said, "Clear on that. Why don't you bring Borden with you? The kids would like her, I'm sure. And Borden seems happy here, too."

This was true. His cat still wasn't keen on the cottage or the forest beyond the windows.

"I'll do that." He rolled out of bed, went to give the librarian a kiss. "For the record, I like it here, too," he whispered, his mouth against her ear.

"Oh, do you?" Charlotte pushed him back, then stepped into a skirt. For some reason she always dressed in the most dowdy clothes for work. But he wouldn't complain. Not when he knew what she looked like without those clothes.

In the ensuite bathroom he grimaced at his reflection. He'd grown fond of his longish hair.

Charlotte's gaze was amused, as she reached around him for her hair brush. "Is your vanity getting the better of your curiosity?"

She knew him too well. How had that happened? They'd been sleeping together for only a few months. But she was right, of course. Birdie's amnesia had him fascinated. Was it genuine?

Maybe it was. By all accounts the accident had been horrific and she'd suffered a terrible blow to the head.

But—what if she'd been running from something, looking for a clean start. Pretending to have amnesia would give her the perfect opportunity to start over.

Problem with that, of course, was constantly having to be on your guard in case you inadvertently gave yourself away.

* * *

When he did go for a haircut—which was rarely—Dougal preferred a regular barbershop. Not a fancy day spa with cucumber infused drinking water and a tropical rainforest soundtrack.

But today he was going to make an exception.

He opened the door of Skin Deep and was immediately cocooned in a scent that was soft and herbal. Not too sweet. Kind of nice, actually.

He went to the counter, where a well-coifed young woman was manning the appointment book.

At her raised eyebrows, he said, "I don't have an appointment, but I was hoping to get a haircut today."

"You're in luck. I think Belle can squeeze you in. Let me go back and check."

While he was waiting a woman in her forties came to the counter to pay for her treatment. Even Dougal could tell that the reason she looked stunning was almost entirely due to her hair style.

A moment later, he realized the woman was Alicia Arden, the mayor's wife.

She did a double-take. "Dougal Lachlan? The author?"

He shrugged.

"I love your books! Say, would you consider attending my next book club meeting? Your latest was our January selection. I know the other ladies would love to ask you some questions about your process."

"I don't do book clubs," he said bluntly.

"I'd love it if you'd make an exception and do mine."

Her eyes narrowed in that speculative, womanly way he was used to seeing late at night in a barroom.

She was just pressing her card into his hand, when the receptionist returned and told him Belle was ready for him.

He raised his eyebrows at the mayor's wife, left her comment unanswered, and gladly went to meet Belle.

For many years his mom had worked as a cleaner at Skin Deep, and Belle greeted him with a big hug. A cloud of perfume engulfed him, along with her skinny, but strong arms.

"You're finally home! Your mother would be so glad." She smiled at him, no trace of accusation in her heavily made-up, cat-shaped, eyes.

"You look good, Belle. Haven't changed a bit."

"It's been a long time, Dougal." She smiled. "You always knew just the right thing to say."

She took his arm. "Come here to the sinks. We have a new girl doing shampoos today. Birdie, take good care of this man for me, please. He's Twisted Cedars' most famous author."

Belle left then, to check on one of her other clients.

Dougal took a good look at the woman presiding over the shampoo chairs.

Very pretty, even with the mottled purple bruising around her big blue eyes. Her nose was straight and slender, her upper lip an exaggerated bow. Her long, strawberry blonde hair looked thick and healthy in a simple ponytail. And as she folded a towel over the edge of the sink, he noticed she had long, slender fingers with turquoise polished nails.

Aside from the bruising, she looked like a normal, attractive woman.

But when her gaze met his, Dougal felt a jolt. Almost like recognition. Or was it sympathy? He'd interviewed a lot of victims in his life. But he'd never met anyone who had such an aura of sadness about them.

While he'd been studying her, she, too, had been looking at him.

"I feel like I know you."

"Do you like to read true crime stories?"

"I'm not sure. I was in an accident on Friday. I can't remember much just yet."

"I heard. My girlfriend, Charlotte Hammond, gave you a tour of the town last night."

"Oh, yes. She was so kind."

"She mentioned you're suffering from amnesia. Do you really not remember who you are?"

"I do have memories. But they're all jumbled." Birdie continued to look at him as if trying to work out a puzzle. "You asked if I read true crime stories. Is that what you write?"

"Yes. My name is Dougal Lachlan. I've—"

"Oh! I do remember you. You're one of my favorite authors. I can't believe I'm actually meeting you in person."

"I'm flattered." He studied her eyes, trying to read the motivations concealed within them. As far as he could tell, she wasn't faking anything right now. "I mean, you've forgotten so much, yet you recognize my name."

"I can't explain it. Random things will just pop into my head. I can't control what I remember, though. I wish I could."

She asked him to sit, then. "I'd better get busy or I'll lose my job."

Reluctantly he took a seat. "Don't put any smelly goop in my hair."

"We have unscented products for clients with allergies. I'll use those."

After checking the temperature of the water, she shampooed his hair, giving him a damned-good scalp massage at the same time. As Birdie was wrapping a towel around his neck, he noticed a tattoo on her wrist.

"What's that "O" mean?"

"No idea."

Their glances met in the mirror, and, again, he saw no guile in her eyes.

"So do you think you'll stay in Twisted Cedars long?"

"I-I don't know. I'm hoping I'll remember who I am and where I belong soon."

"It must be terrifying to have your entire past wiped clean."

"Yes. But sometimes I wonder if it would be more terrifying to remember."

"Do you think you were running from someone who wanted to hurt you?"

She shrugged. "That's what the police asked me. But I don't know the answer."

Belle came by and gave her a pleased smile. "Thank you, Birdie. I'll take him now."

And then Dougal had to submit to Belle's prodding as she went to work on his hair, first combing it, then running her fingers through it, and finally cutting off more than he was comfortable with.

"So are you still working on that book about the four librarians who were strangled with red scarves?" Belle asked as she worked.

"You heard about that?"

Belle laughed. "I hear about everything."

She pulled out the hair dryer then, and then after his hair was dry, finished it off with a spritz of some product and a final fluffing with her fingers. "Charlotte's going to like this. You wait and see."

* * *

Dougal stepped outside, noted his well-coifed reflection in the shop window, and immediately ran his fingers through his hair, shaking his head at the same time. If he'd been a dog, he'd have found a nice plot of dirt to roll around in.

But he didn't go that far.

Hell. Never again was he letting anyone near him with a tube of gel or a hair dryer.

Dougal welcomed the wind coming off the ocean as he walked back to Charlotte's to get his car. But he was afraid that not even a strong breeze would get his hair back to the carefree, rumpled look that he favored.

As he drove out toward the Librarian Cottage, a slow unease began burrowing into his gut. He hadn't gone this long with a book contract since he'd sold his first novel nine years ago. It was fine to talk about shifting from true crime to mystery fiction. But unless he wrote a synopsis and three damn good chapters, he wasn't getting an advance, or a contract. Period.

Just yesterday he'd had calls from both his agent and his editor.

They didn't like the new direction.

Was he really sure he wanted to leave New York? And write fiction?

He didn't know. Only that for sure he wasn't going to write about those four murdered librarians the way Monty had tried to goad him into doing. The very idea of chronicling his father's crimes made him sick.

It was also maddening that the entire town seemed to know about those murders. He should have been more circumspect when he was doing his research. He normally was.

But meeting Charlotte had changed something inside of himself. He'd enjoyed talking to her. And had opened up far more than normal. About everything, not just his writing.

The five mile drive went by all too quickly and as Dougal approached the cottage, he had to acknowledge one truth.

Moving here hadn't been a mistake. Charlotte was part of the reason. But also, he really loved living out here in the woods.

When he rounded the final grove of trees, though, he was dismayed to see Liz Brook's rusted-out, green jeep parked out front.

He'd forgotten she was due to clean this Tuesday. He hoped she hadn't freaked out his cat. And that she was almost finished.

His mother had cleaned other people's houses for a living. Now that he was on the other side, paying the dough so someone else would scrub his toilet, it felt weird.

In New York his apartment had been so small he'd never bothered with a cleaner. But when he'd decided to move into the Librarian Cottage, the place had been uninhabited for several decades. The dust and grime had been more than he even he could tolerate. And after hiring Liz that first time, it had felt cheap not to give her a regular gig.

He'd just gotten out of his car when the petite, dark-haired young woman emerged from the front door with two buckets, both filled with cleaning supplies.

She set them on the porch so she could close the door behind her. "Good timing. I just finished."

"Thanks." He felt guilty now, for having had bad thoughts about her. She looked tired. She was a little thing for such hard labor. And she was young. Mid-twenties at the most. "It's a warm one. Want a beer?"

She looked at her watch, and frowned, then surprised him by saying, "Sure."

He immediately regretted his impulsive invitation. Now he was going to have to sit and make polite conversation for at least fifteen minutes when, if he'd just kept his mouth shut, she would have been gone by now.

"Make yourself comfortable." He indicated one of the wicker chairs on the porch. "I'll be right back." He grabbed two lagers from the fridge, not bothering with any glasses. Back outside he twisted the top off hers first, then his own.

What the hell were they going to talk about?

"Where did you say you moved here from again, Liz?"

She'd taken her hair out of the ponytail she'd been wearing while she worked, and her brown curls were everywhere. She pushed them off her forehead, which he could see was damp with sweat.

"I never said. I've moved around a lot."

"In Oregon, though?"

"Yup. It was just me and my Mom. She's a coke addict. Living on the streets in Portland, last I saw her." She raised her chin as she said this, daring him to feel sorry for her.

He recognized the bravado. And respected it.

His childhood must have been a picnic compared to hers. They'd been poor, and his mother had had a habit he detested of indulging in one-night stands with men who weren't good enough to hold a door open for her. But his mom had been kind, never raised her voice or a hand at him, though God knows he'd given her provocation.

And while it had only been a trailer, she'd kept a roof over their heads. And meals on the table.

"Liking Twisted Cedars so far?"

"It's as good as anywhere else. First time I've cleaned houses for a living. I like it. Never did care for having a boss look over my shoulder."

He'd never thought someone could enjoy cleaning houses for a living. He'd always assumed his mother didn't. But she hadn't complained about going to work, ever, that he could remember.

Could it be his mother had enjoyed the job, too?

He liked to think it might have been true.

"But don't you get clients who blame you for breaking stuff you know you didn't? Or fussing about how you missed dusting the top shelf of the china cabinet?"

Liz shrugged. "Those kind of people are easy to handle. It's just a power play. I do a good job and I let them know I won't put up with that shit."

He laughed. "Good for you."

She looked a little embarrassed then. She set down the beer bottle, started to get up, then settled back down. "A lot of my clients still talk about your Mom. They really cared about her."

Dougal's throat closed up. He still had a hard time admitting to himself she was really gone.

When he'd found out his mom had cancer, that she was going to die, he'd taken her and Jamie on a trip to Hawaii. That was the last time he'd seen her. He hadn't been able to face going home for his mother's last awful month. Then he'd skipped the funeral, because why the hell would he come home for that, when he hadn't been here to say good-bye?

Dougal pressed the cool beer bottle up to his forehead. "Mom was special. She didn't deserve a shit son like me."

"You loved her. That's something."

True. But had she known? He'd never said it.

"She knew." Liz set down her unfinished beer, then grabbed the buckets. "I better get going. Mayor's house is next."

He went to help her with the supplies, but she waved him off. "It's easier when I'm balanced."

"Suit yourself."

"I try to, whenever I can." She gave him a salute as she drove off with her windows down and rock music blaring.

chapter fifteen

at six-thirty, silver-haired Ben Mason stopped by Jamie's office. He was the elder of the partners, with a courtly, elegant manner about him.

"Still here? It's a beautiful night. I'm off to play a round of golf. We have an opening if you'd like to join us?"

It was Ben's contention that a solid golf game was important to build client relations. "One of these days I'll take you up on that, Ben. But I'm meeting someone in forty minutes."

She lowered her gaze to the file in her hands. She shouldn't have to hide the fact that she was having dinner with Kyle. But she suspected Ben would disapprove.

"That's too bad. See you in the morning, then." He hesitated before adding, "Sure is nice to have you back."

"Thank you." It was good to hear, that was for sure.

Ten minutes later, Jamie was on her way to Brookings to meet Kyle far away from the prying eyes of their family, friends and neighbors. She'd suggested a family-style restaurant just off the highway, knowing the bright lighting and cheerful wait staff would make her feel safe.

Not that she was afraid of Kyle. She wasn't. But it couldn't hurt to be extra cautious.

She asked for a table near the window, so she could enjoy the ocean view as she waited. She was fifteen minutes early and Kyle typically ran late, so it might be a while. She ordered a glass of pinot noir, and had to resist the urge to guzzle it when it arrived.

Her marriage had imploded in less than two months and she no longer had a home. She couldn't keep staying with Stella and Amos. But where should she go? She wished she hadn't sold the trailer. But the deal had gone through, the money was in her bank account and Liz Brooks was now living in the only home Jamie had ever known.

Maybe it was time she bought her own place. A real house with a foundation that couldn't be moved. She had a good job, and a healthy down payment. One thing was for sure though—she wouldn't use Quinpool Realty as her broker.

The ocean side windows of the restaurant were all open, and Jamie could feel the warm Pacific breeze dance over her face and down her arms. Summer was fleeting on the Pacific Coast and it was hard not to feel that she was missing out on this one.

In her alternative life, the one she'd thought she was going to have, she and Kyle would be just home from their honeymoon. They would have biked across the Golden Gate Bridge, gone hiking in the Muir Woods, and sipped wine at outdoor cafés in the Sonoma Valley.

The sound of an incoming text message pulled her out of her pity party. It was from Stella.

GRILLING PRAWNS FOR DINNER.

Oh crap, she'd forgotten to tell Stella her plans. SORRY STELLA. WON'T BE HOME UNTIL LATER.

WORKING LATE?

I WAS. NOW WAITING TO MEET KYLE.

GOOD IDEA?

It was starting to feel less and less so. Jamie's stomach was churning with nerves. The wine hadn't helped. Maybe she should leave. Kyle could say everything he needed over the phone.

But then she saw him. Her husband—and he was still that, despite everything—was looking straight at her and walking this way. He was pale, maybe a few pounds thinner than the last time she saw him. But he was still handsome, in the way that blond men with blue eyes and great smiles often were.

And he was smiling now, though his eyes looked nervous.

"Good to see you, Jamie."

She wished, oh how she wished, she could say the same. Instead, all she did was nod.

He stepped forward as if to hug her, but she glanced down at the table and after an awkward pause, he took the vacant chair. Not that long ago, his touch had thrilled her. But she couldn't stand to think about that now.

"How are you doing?"

She sighed. "How do you think?"

"I know," he said quickly. "It's been awful. And I'm so sorry."

Was he? She studied his eyes. She thought she could see remorse, but he'd fooled her before.

"I'm glad you agreed to meet. I need to explain what happened. I'm not a monster, Jamie."

"I didn't come for an explanation. It's too late for that. We need to...start proceedings."

He winced. "You're sure?"

Had he really thought she might stay? She leaned forward, counting his infractions on her fingers. "You lied about Olivia retiring so I would quit my job and come work for you. You lied about your business trips. And most of all you lied about Daisy—and what you did to her."

"I never meant to hurt her. What happened that night— it's become a blur. But I can tell you in all honesty that I meant her no harm."

"What did happen that night?"

"I'd like to tell you. But my lawyer has advised me to keep quiet."

"Even now you don't think I deserve the truth?"

"Of course you do. I'm telling you what matters. That I never intended to hurt her."

"So it just happened? She just fell and hit her head?"

Kyle sat there, neither denying nor confirming.

"If it was an accident, if you didn't mean her harm, why didn't you call 911?"

He took a deep breath. "I panicked. But I wasn't trying to protect myself. I was thinking about the twins and what would happen to them if..." He closed his eyes briefly. Took a deep breath. "Yes, I was stupid. And disrespectful to Daisy. I've wished a thousand times that I could have a do-over for that night."

"Easy for you to say now."

"You know what Chester and Cory mean to me. I couldn't stand for them to lose their mother and their father—both on the same night."

The misery in his voice was reflected in his eyes. He'd made a lot of mistakes, and he seemed ready to admit that much, at least.

And she was also inclined to believe he hadn't intended to hurt Daisy. She did believe he genuinely loved his children. But had he ever loved her?

The more she looked back on their relationship, the more she doubted that he had.

When his mother left his father and moved away, he'd needed a new caregiver and homemaker. That's all she'd been to him. And that had to be why he'd tried to manipulate her into leaving her job.

The server came and they both ordered the grilled fish special.

A few minutes later, Jamie asked, "What's going to happen?"

"My lawyer thinks they're going to arrest me and charge me for manslaughter."

She could see the fear in his eyes and hear it in his voice. "What will that mean?"

"Ten years in jail," Kyle said bluntly. "If I'm convicted."

As the server approached with their food, they fell quiet. When they were alone again, Kyle continued. "If it was only me, I wouldn't care so much. I'm willing to do the time. Believe me, I feel horrible about what happened."

Unshed tears glistened in his eyes. But were they genuine? Jamie broke off studying Kyle's face and stared numbly at the drink and the food on the table. She couldn't touch any of it. Part of her believed him. Part of her even sympathized with his dilemma.

But she couldn't let him win her over. She had to harden her heart and remember Daisy, who hadn't deserved to die.

And Charlotte, Daisy's sister, who had been entitled to the truth, not live all these years with the futile hope that one day Daisy would come back to Twisted Cedars.

Never mind the poor twins.

"Were your parents in on the cover-up?"

Now Kyle's gaze dropped to the table.

She supposed he was protecting them. Because if they'd known and had failed to report the crime to the authorities, they were guilty, too.

"Is this why your parents got divorced? Your mother wanted you to tell the truth. But you and your dad overruled her. She stayed until the guilt got to be too much. Then she left her marriage and moved to Portland."

Kyle blinked, then took a deep breath. "Actually, Mom's living in Sacramento, Jamie. I know it looks bad. But my parents both know I didn't mean to harm Daisy. That's all they cared about. If you could believe it, too, that would mean a lot to me."

He put his hands on the table, palms upward, an invitation for her to touch him. But she wouldn't. Couldn't.

"Getting together like this, wasn't a good idea."

"God, Jamie, you being so cold and distant is killing me. I'm the same guy you fell in love with."

"That's not true. I'm afraid you never were the guy I fell in love with." She picked up her purse, intending to leave money for her share of the food, but Kyle waved her away.

"Don't add insult to injury. I'll pay."

She stood, slung her purse strap over her shoulder. "You'll be hearing from my lawyer soon." She swallowed the lump rising in her throat. "Good luck, Kyle."

chapter sixteen

S tella," Dougal said, "I need you to tell me about my father."

Her face, so familiar to him in the way that anyone's grandmother or aunt's face is familiar, looked stricken.

Stella and her husband Amos weren't blood relatives, but Dougal had grown up having Sunday dinners at their house. As long as he could remember his mother, sister and he had spent Christmas here, Thanksgiving, too. When he was in sixth grade, Amos had helped him build a tree house. Through the kitchen window, Dougal could see it standing still, in the old oak at the back of the yard.

"You know all you need to about your old man." Stella took a cloth and dried her hands. He'd caught her doing the dinner dishes. Just one plate—neither Amos nor his sister had come home for the meal.

Amos was working in his shop, Stella had said. And his sister, well, she'd agreed to meet with Kyle.

Dougal couldn't believe it. When he'd found Daisy's body buried behind the Librarian Cottage he'd felt one good thing might come from the tragedy, that Jamie would finally be done with the asshole she'd made the mistake of marrying.

Not too many people knew Kyle as well as Dougal did. They'd grown up together, hung out throughout high school, played football and partied together.

He knew the inner workings of Kyle Quinpool's mind. And they were selfish, entitled and egotistical.

Maybe his sister was meeting him to iron out details of a separation. That was a hopeful thought.

Dougal stepped away from the window. There were still pictures of himself and Jamie, as kids, on Stella's fridge. She and Amos hadn't had children of their own, and they'd doted on him and his sister.

"Stella, I'd love nothing better than to forget Ed Lachlan ever existed. But he won't let me. When I went back to the city to pack up my apartment, I found out he'd been my neighbor for half-a-year, under an assumed name."

"What? You mean he moved there after he got out of prison?"

"Over the years he's tried phoning me and emailing me and even writing me letters. I don't know why he's so damned determined to establish a connection between us. I've made it very clear I want nothing to do with him."

"You didn't recognize him?"

"Why would I? I was a little kid last time I saw him. Plus he's old now. Looks about ten years older than he should."

"So where is he now?"

"God only knows. He's taken off again. I'll bet he's got a new identity as well."

"Good. Maybe this time he'll stay gone."

"I wish I could believe that."

If he could, he'd let Stella be. He knew she had a deep aversion to discussing Edward Lachlan—partly because she wanted to protect him and Jamie from the truth about their father. But also because she felt guilty that she and Amos had been the ones to introduce Edward to his mother.

"But given his track record, it isn't likely. He's going to be getting touch with me again, Stella. I just don't know how he'll do it this time."

"You have to keep avoiding him."

"The best way for me to protect myself—and Jamie—is to find out everything I can about him. Knowledge is what I need. I can't afford to hide my head in the sand."

After Liz had left the cottage that afternoon, Dougal had tried to settle down to write an outline for his new idea.

But the only stories in his head were those of the four librarians who had been murdered by his father.

Why had Ed Lachlan killed them? Was it just a way of seeking revenge on his birth mother for giving him up? If so, it was monstrous. And Dougal needed to understand what had made his father capable of such evilness.

Not so he could write a book the way his father wanted him to. But so he could put the ghosts to rest. And hopefully move on.

Stella sank into a kitchen chair, then glanced at her watch. "We don't have much time. Liz is coming over in half an hour to go over our schedule for the next month. And your sister will be home soon as well."

"We have enough time to make a start," he insisted. "Can I get you something to drink?"

"God, Dougal, you always were a persistent little bugger." She started rubbing her lower back and he felt guilty. She worked hard. She didn't deserve to be interrogated like this.

But he had to know.

"It's hot in here," Stella opened the back screen door. "Let's go out on the patio. Maybe you should bring a couple of beers."

He found two cans in the fridge and brought them out. The sun was low and long shadows extended past the height of the shrubs and trees, shrouding the yard in darkness.

Stella took a long drink, then stared dully at the old oak. He suspected it was the past she was looking into—not the gnarled wood and weathered branches. As her expression grew duller and sadder, he knew he was right.

"We first met your father when he was working with Amos at the Golf and Country Club. Ed had been hired on to help Amos build the new clubhouse. One skill your father had was the ability to switch charm on and off like an electrical switch. And for some reason he decided he would befriend my Amos."

Dougal had heard this part before. But he sat still and listened.

"One night, Amos decided to invite Ed home for dinner. And me, I figured I would round out the numbers and invite my new business partner, too. Your mother and I met at the Ocean View Motel, but neither of us were happy working there, so we decided to form a partnership and start our own cleaning company."

Dougal decided it was time for a little re-direction. "What do you know about his past, Stella? Did he ever tell you where he was born? Or anything about his parents?"

"He said he moved here from Salem. He did mention the fact that he'd been adopted, and that they'd been cruel people. Amos saw the scars on his back once. So Ed wasn't lying about that. When he was sixteen he ran away from those folks."

Dougal pulled his notepad and pen from the back pocket of his jeans and scratched down the information. "Who were his adoptive parents? Did he mention their names?"

"God, I can't remember Dougal. But they must have lived on a farm or at least an acreage. He mentioned once how there were no neighbors to see or hear what his adoptive parents were doing to him."

An icy chill raced down Dougal's back. "When did he move to Twisted Cedars?"

"He'd been around for a few years before he started working with Amos. Working with a roofing company, I believe."

Dougal needed dates. "Mom married him in 1977 and I was born the same year. They were together six months before that, so they must have met in 1976."

"That's the year they built the clubhouse," Stella agreed.

"So if you were to pick a year Edward moved to Twisted Cedars...?" There was a sound from the side of the house, a rustling, but Stella didn't seem to notice.

"I'd guess your father must have moved here in 1972 or '73."

"It was 1972. When I moved into the Librarian Cottage, Charlotte found an old letter addressed to her aunt from an adoption agency in Portland."

Stella looked puzzled. "An adoption agency?"

"Yes. They were warning Shirley their offices had been broken into and some of their records stolen—including the adoption documents for her son."

Stella sucked in a surprised breath. "Are you telling me Shirley Hammond was your father's birth mother?"

"I'm almost positive. Here's what I do know for sure. Shirley got pregnant when she was sixteen-years-old and gave the child up for adoption. I can't prove that child was my father, but I'm pretty sure that Ed, at least, believed he was her son."

Stella placed a hand on her heart, and at that moment, Liz Brooks appeared from the same side of the house as he'd heard the rustling sound earlier. Her dark, curly hair was loose, and she wore faded jean shorts, a T-shirt and plain rubber flip-flops on her tiny feet.

How long had she been there, standing in the shadows on the side of the house?

"Liz. You startled me, dear. I'll get you a drink. Beer okay?"

When she nodded, Stella disappeared inside to get the drink.

Liz moved closer to Dougal. "You were talking about Edward Lachlan."

"We were," he agreed. "And you were listening."

Liz fingered a pendant hanging at her throat. She had to be in her mid-twenties, but she looked so young in that moment, almost like a teenager.

"Here we go." Stella was back. She handed Liz the cool can and invited her to sit down. "Dougal will be leaving soon. Then we can discuss our business."

"I'm sorry I interrupted your conversation." Liz's voice sounded strained. "I actually think I have something to contribute."

"But we were talking about Dougal's father, dear. You've never met him."

"That's true. But my father did."

"Your father knew Edward Lachlan?"

"They met in prison. And Ed told my father lots of stories." She nodded at Dougal. "Mostly about you."

chapter seventeen

It was almost eight o'clock when Wade got home from Sacramento. He thought about parking himself in front of the TV for a few hours before he went to bed. Instead, he drove by the women's emergency shelter, intending to make a quick check, for his own peace of mind.

When he arrived, he got out of his SUV, intending to check in with the night staff. On his way to the visitor's entrance, however, he caught a whiff of cigarette smoke. He turned toward the designated outdoor smoking area.

Birdie was sitting alone, a cigarette in her hands.

He approached her slowly, not wanting to alarm her. "You may not remember me—"

"I do. You're the Sheriff."

She was looking a lot better than the last time he'd seen her. A lot better.

"Yes. Name's Wade MacKay. Mind if I join you for a few minutes?"

"Go ahead."

He settled into one of the plastic chairs. Shrubs protected them from the main road to the east. A trellis screen blocked them off on the north and west, and the building was to the south. It was a private seating area designed to make women feel safe as they indulged in their smokes.

"How are you feeling?"

"A lot better. I even found a job. Today was my first day."

"A job?" He sure hadn't expected to hear that.

"I'm a hair stylist."

"So you've got your memory back?"

"Only fragments. I'm a hair stylist, and I'm pretty sure I used to live in a city, not a small town or the country. I like

Thai food and the color orange." She smiled sadly, then shrugged. "Not much, is it?"

He glanced at the cigarette. So far she hadn't taken a single drag. "And that?"

"I thought maybe I smoked, but I took a puff and it made me cough. So I guess I don't." She ground the cigarette into a large can filled with sand.

"Give it time. I bet you'll remember more tomorrow."

"I still have no idea why I was in that man's truck. Or even if I knew him." She stared out into the night. "I should at least be sorry he's dead, shouldn't I? But I don't feel anything."

"You've had a bad shock. Physically and mentally. I wouldn't be too hard on myself, if I was you."

"*Boldness be my friend.*"

"What's that?"

"I'm not sure. I was thinking I had to stop feeling so scared about the future and those words just came to me."

"Anyone in your situation would be scared." Only four days ago this woman sitting across from him would have been living her regular life. Now she had no idea who she was or where she'd come from. "But you're safe here. Try to relax."

"I'd like to. But I can't help feeling as if there is something important I need to be doing."

Was this another memory, trying to break through?

"But the harder I try to remember what it is, the more my head aches." Birdie reached a hand to her scar and touched it gently. "What if I never remember?"

He had no answer for her. He couldn't even imagine being in her shoes. To be himself, but to have no memories of Twisted Cedars, or his job, parents, or any of his friends. Who would that person be?

* * *

Jamie thought about the twins as she drove home from her meeting with Kyle. Charlotte had told her that when they drove out to the summer camp to tell them about their mother, they'd claimed to already know she was dead.

Was it possible they'd also known their father was responsible? They'd only been toddlers the night their mother died. But maybe they'd heard things. Kids often knew more than adults suspected they did.

It was awful to think of Chester and Cory carrying such heavy burdens.

Jamie's route home took her right by the Hammond's house. She was tempted to stop and say hi to the children. But they needed to get used to the routine of living with Charlotte.

So Jamie took a right turn into town, drove a few blocks, then turned right again. A group of pine trees growing in a vacant lot reminded her of the woods at the back of the Librarian Cottage. She thought of Daisy, buried and forgotten all those years.

How could he have done that?

He was a monster. He had to be.

And yet—she thought of how patient and gentle he could be with the children. In bed he'd been giving and loving. And he always made the time to listen when she needed to talk about missing her mother or being upset with her brother.

What advice would her mother give, if she were alive? Would she tell her to have her marriage annulled, to cut her losses, not to worry about children who weren't hers to worry about?

No.

Jamie knew her mother had retained an attachment to her father, even though he'd been abusive toward her. She suspected her Mom had kicked him out because she was worried for Dougal, and for the unborn child who had been Jamie, not for herself.

Why else had she found a letter from her father in her mother's possessions after she died last year?

Besides, it hadn't been in her mother's character to hate or dismiss anyone. She'd had the most loving heart of anyone Jamie had ever met.

Having reached the small bungalow where Stella and Amos lived, Jamie turned off the ignition and car lights. Now that it was almost nine, the air was finally cooling off. The gentle breeze carried summertime scents of backyard barbecues and blooming gardens.

The lights were off inside Stella and Amos's house, but Jamie could hear voices coming from the backyard. She followed the paved path along the side of the house, her arms brushing against the lilac hedge that separated this property from the neighbor's.

When she emerged from around the corner, she was surprised to see three people sitting on the plastic patio furniture.

"I didn't know you were having a party, Stella."

But the only festive element to the gathering was the fact that all three of them—Stella, her brother and Liz Brooks—had a beer in their hands. Their expressions were grim, and no one had bothered to light the outdoor candles or to set out any munchies.

"Grab a drink," Dougal said. "I think you'll need it."

"What in the world were you guys talking about?" She'd heard their voices earlier, but they'd clammed up the moment they saw her.

Liz was so small she was able to sit cross-legged in her chair. Jamie remembered Stella saying she and Liz were planning to have a business meeting tonight. But she didn't think Dougal would be much interested in that subject.

"Would you like a drink, dear?"

Before Stella could get out of her chair, Jamie indicated she should remain where she was. It seemed everyone was very anxious that she have a beer, so she might as well oblige them. She filled a bowl with potato chips, too. Not having eaten much of her dinner, she was suddenly starving.

Back outside, the tension seemed even thicker than before.

Was this an ambush?

Had Stella told Dougal she was meeting Kyle?

But that didn't explain Liz's presence.

"Would someone please tell me what's going on here?"

"Liz?" Dougal said.

"Jamie, I was just telling your brother something that I should have told you both when I first moved here. But I was afraid you'd think I was some kind of weird stalker. So I kept quiet. I thought it might get easier once we got to know one another a little better."

"I don't get it." Jamie studied Stella's face, then Dougal's for a clue.

"Liz's father met ours in prison. I guess they were sort of buddies."

Jamie blinked at him, surprise robbing her of words.

"Liz was just telling us a bit about her past. The truth this time."

Liz looked a little sheepish. "I grew up in foster care. People were always asking for my so-called story. I figured it wasn't their business, so why should I tell them what really happened?"

"Fair enough," Jamie supposed.

"My Mom wasn't a coke-addict." Liz glanced at Dougal. "She was actually a really good mother. But she died when I was young."

Dougal's eyes softened. "What about your dad?"

Liz lowered her gaze, as well as her voice. "He was in jail."

"What did he do?" Jamie asked, finally getting her equilibrium back.

"He got drunk and picked a fight at a bar. And he killed the guy."

"And he served his time with our father?"

"Part of it. He actually got out a few years before your dad. I was twenty at the time, on my own. I'd learned not to give a rat's ass what other people thought of me. So when dad asked if he could live with me, I said yes."

"Sit down, Jamie. We have an extra chair." Stella pointed.

Jamie did as told.

Then her brother indicated her beer. "And if you're going to keep your mouth open like that, you might as well pour some of that into it."

Obligingly she took a sip. "Was it just a coincidence that you moved to Twisted Cedars and took a job with our Mom?"

"No. Dad was full of stories about Ed when he got out. Your father made quite the impression. Dad said no one could tell a story like Ed. What he liked to talk about most, though, was his son."

Dougal sank a little into his chair.

"He was so proud of you," Liz said. "He read all your books over and over, then he'd re-tell the stories to the other prisoners. He said that one day you were going to write a book about him, and then you'd both be famous."

"Christ." Dougal looked disgusted.

"Another thing he talked about a lot was this wonderful town, Twisted Cedars. He said he'd never been happier than when he lived here, and he told my Dad that when he got out of prison he'd meet him here and they'd start up a construction business together."

"But your dad never came to our town?" Jamie guessed.

"No. He was sick when he got out of prison. He only lived a few months. But he told me I should come here. I guess I was curious. Was any place really as wonderful as Dad seemed to think this town was? I had nothing tying me down after Dad died. So I kind of made it a pilgrimage. Even sprinkled some of his ashes by those two cedar trees downtown."

Jamie felt her throat thicken. "Why didn't you tell me this sooner?"

"I hadn't known Stella and your Mom long before the topic of Ed Lachlan came up. And it was pretty clear how much Stella hated him. Maybe your mom, too, I couldn't tell."

Jamie thought of the letter her mother had saved. "No. I don't think she hated him."

"Well, Stella did."

"Damn right." Stella's tone brokered no doubt on the subject.

"So I kept my mouth shut. And then I started hearing how Dougal wanted to know more about his father, so I thought I would tell my story. Even though it isn't much, I guess."

"It's good you told us," Dougal said.

"Yes," Jamie agreed. "It's nice to know that there were people who liked our father."

"You would see it that way." Dougal looked at her with a brotherly mixture of contempt and fondness.

"I keep telling you, he isn't all bad." Jamie thought about Kyle. "No one is."

chapter eighteen

Charlotte was in bed when she heard Dougal's car pull into her driveway. Since Borden was sleeping sprawled over her legs, she waited for him to let himself in.

"Hey, Char. It's been a hell of a night." He stripped his T-shirt and tossed it on the chair, then unbuttoned his jeans.

She set down *Pride and Prejudice*, to enjoy the view.

Dougal didn't work out regularly, not in a gym, at least. But his body was lean and well-muscled, all the same. Then she noticed something else. "Nice haircut."

He scrubbed his hands through his hair as if trying to rid himself from fleas. "Belle sprayed this guck on it. I can't wait to have my shower tomorrow morning."

"Did you see Birdie?"

"She shampooed my hair."

"And? What did you think?"

"Felt sorry for her, actually. Her memory loss seems legit. There is something sort of compelling about her, isn't there."

Charlotte felt the slightest ping of jealousy. "She's very beautiful."

"Yeah. But that's not it." He picked up the book she'd just set aside. "Jane Austen?"

"You're not a fan?"

"Oh contraire." He put a hand to his throat. "*In vain I have struggled. It will not do. My feelings will not be repressed. You must allow me to tell you how ardently I admire and love you.*"

Charlotte burst out laughing. Never would she have guessed Dougal could quote from *Pride and Prejudice*. "Don't stop," she said, when she had control of her voice.

"But this is where you tell me I've got my head up my ass and you wouldn't marry me if I was the last person on earth."

"Jane says it so much more eloquently. *I had not known you a month before I felt that you were the last man in the world whom I could ever be prevailed on to marry.*"

This time Dougal was the one to chuckle. "I see I've met my match."

"I've only read the book about twenty times. And watched the movie at least that often. How do you explain your fluency?"

"Last year I helped a friend with her lines. She was trying for the part of Elizabeth Bennett in an off-Broadway play. Have to say it was a lot of fun."

He sat on her side of the bed and gave Borden a scratch on the neck. "Nice to see the two of you curled up together. Kids asleep?"

"At least an hour ago."

"And the back door—why was it unlocked?"

"For you, obviously."

"Maybe you should give me a key."

"Looking for more commitment?"

"Right. That, plus I'd rather you and the kids were safe at night."

"A minute ago you're declaring your ardent love. Now you don't want commitment?" She stopped teasing. "Honestly, Dougal, this is Twisted Cedars. We're safe."

"For a woman who is scared of crowds, the dark, and speaking in public, you're awfully blasé about this. But you've got to promise me you'll be more careful. Lock the doors, Char. I'm serious."

Her home, and this town, had always felt like sanctuaries to Charlotte. It was the rest of the world that was scary.

But now that the children were living with her, Dougal was right, she shouldn't take any chances. "Okay. I will."

"I hope you mean that." He gave Borden one last pat, then crawled under the covers with her. "Mmm. I like what you wore to bed."

Which was nothing.

And led, quite quickly, to something. With a disgusted sniff, Borden jumped off the bed and retreated to someplace quieter.

* * *

Charlotte loved being held by Dougal after they'd made love. He pulled her head to rest on his chest, and then teased his fingers up and down her back in the most delightful way.

At some point Borden returned to the room. She resumed her position on the bed, gave them a baleful look, then curled into the space between their feet.

"I don't think Borden approves of our sex life."

"It's not her approval I'm looking for." He gave her ass a suggestive rub.

She laughed and pushed his hand away. "You haven't told me how things went with Stella, tonight. Did she tell you anything more about your father?"

"Cripes, have I got loads to tell you."

"Oh? Should I get up? Pour some drinks?"

"Come back here." He pulled her tightly into his arms. "The big news didn't come from Stella. But let me tell this in order. When I asked about my father, all Stella had to say was that he was originally from Salem. Probably raised on a farm, or an acreage, where neighbors couldn't hear the abuse that went on. He finally ran away for good when he was sixteen."

"Sounds rough. Not surprising when you consider how he turned out, I suppose."

"I haven't told you the interesting part yet. Liz Brooks came by while Stella and I were discussing dear old dad and she dropped a big confession on us."

Charlotte pushed herself up so she could see Dougal's face. "What does Liz have to do with any of this?"

"Turns out she had a secret connection to Ed—or at least her father did. They were in prison together."

"Well that's kind of weird."

"I guess Ed turned on the charm in prison, told lots of stories, had everyone hanging on his every word. He talked Twisted Cedars up big. Told Liz's father that when they got out they'd move here and start a business together."

"So did Liz's dad ever get here?"

"No. He died before he had the chance. But Liz brought some of his ashes."

Dougal explained more about Liz's reasons for coming here and why she'd kept quiet about the connection for so long.

Then he explained how Ed had told everyone in prison who would listen that his son, the famous author, was going to write a book about him one day.

"Well, this explains a lot. Would have been nice if Liz told you this sooner."

Dougal agreed.

"So what are you going to do next?"

"Tomorrow I go to Salem." He kissed the tip of her nose. "And you make sure you keep that front door locked."

chapter nineteen

five days after the accident

dougal left early for Salem on Wednesday, was out of the house before Charlotte or the twins were awake. Charlotte couldn't help wondering if he would have stayed for breakfast if the kids hadn't been living with her.

They were becoming more comfortable with each other now. Charlotte knew Cory liked her eggs scrambled, Chester preferred them fried. Cory would eat an orange for breakfast, but only if Charlotte peeled off all the white bits. Getting Chester to eat some fruit was more of a challenge. Today she tried him on blueberries.

He wrinkled his nose.

"How are things going at Mrs. Thompson's?" she asked them.

Both kids stared down at their plates.

There had to be a better option. "Want me to sign you up for some fun day camps? We have a whole list at the library. There are camps that focus on arts and crafts, or computers, or sports—whatever you're interested in."

The twins exchanged a knowing look, and when Chester suggested, in a studiously nonchalant tone, "Maybe we could go back to Wolf Creek? It was kind of decent there," Charlotte knew she'd been expertly maneuvered.

But—if it was what they really wanted, why should she deny them?

"Is that what you'd both like?"

Vigorous nodding confirmed that this had been a set up.

"I'll call the director today and see if there are any openings, on one condition." She paused, to make sure they were both paying attention. "Will you tell me the real reason you want to go back to camp? And if that reason is because you're not happy staying here with me, then please just say so. I won't be upset with you. Honestly."

Again the twins shared a look, but this time it was Cory who spoke.

"It's not you, Aunt Charlotte. It's the Thompson kids. They're telling lies about our dad."

"It was easier at the camp," Chester added. "Most of the kids aren't even from Twisted Cedars. And they don't have any TV, newspapers or Internet."

God she hated gossip. No doubt the kids were just repeating what they were hearing at home. "Okay, here's what we'll do. I know this teenaged girl who babysits. Her name is Laila and she's really nice. I'm going to phone her right now."

Fortunately Laila was home, and glad to line up a paying job for the day, that would get her out of the house and helping her Mom look after her younger siblings.

Next Charlotte called Braham Fielding at Wolf Creek Camp. Braham was sympathetic to their predicament.

"I'd be glad to help—they're great kids. In fact we have space right now. When can you get them down here?"

Charlotte consulted with the twins. Their whoops of joy convinced her she was doing the right thing. If she left work early, she could have them there by four.

* * *

By the time she got to work the library felt like a peaceful retreat to Charlotte, despite the fact that she had six toddlers scheduled for a reading circle in an hour. She'd already selected the titles and the books were stacked neatly on her desk.

The familiar titles made her smile. *Mrs. Wishy Washy, Chicka Chicka Boom Boom* and *One Fish Two Fish Red Fish Blue Fish*.

Just before the toddlers arrived, she called Laila to see how she was doing with the twins.

"We're tossing around the football," Laila reported, sounding out of breath. "Then is it okay if we bake some cookies?"

"You've baked cookies before?" Charlotte knew Laila was fourteen—but was that old enough?

"All the time." She sounded very confident.

"Go head. I'm sure the twins will like that." Actually she had no idea if they liked to bake. But she'd be willing to bet they'd be happy to eat the results.

After the reading circle was over, and the moms and children had dispersed throughout the library looking for books to sign out, Charlotte checked her phone for any messages from Dougal.

There was nothing. Probably he was still on the road.

Travel, sudden departures, long absences...Dougal's way of life was not Charlotte's. She preferred schedules and plans and routine. Mysteries, adventures and romances were best enjoyed between the covers of a book.

But somehow, Dougal had shifted her ever so slightly out of her rut. Why, she didn't know. He wasn't her type and she doubted if she was his.

If he would only settle down and work on that novel he was always saying he wanted to write. But since his trip back to New York he'd become even more obsessed with his father and the past. She had no idea where the obsession would lead, or if it would ever really end.

At noon, Charlotte decided to go for a walk, leaving Abigail to handle things at the library. On her mind was a memorial service for her sister. She felt it would provide good closure for the twins—and herself. But with the investigation into Daisy's death going on right now, the timing didn't feel appropriate.

It was sweet that the twins had enjoyed looking at the old family photos of Daisy. But the exercise had underscored to Charlotte how few of their own memories they had of their Mom. They hadn't even been two when Daisy disappeared.

Disappeared. Charlotte had thought of her sister's absence that way for so long, it was hard to adjust to the truth.

Her sister hadn't run off—she'd been killed. Maybe it had been an accident the way Kyle claimed, but technically it was still homicide. Undoubtedly the shock would have been greater if so many years hadn't gone by. In Charlotte's heart, despite the monthly withdrawals from Daisy's bank account, she had known something was wrong.

After her walk, Charlotte returned to work feeling somewhat refreshed. She was catching up with emails when Birdie walked in, wearing a simple black sundress and sunglasses. She looked stunning.

Dougal's line came back to her. *There's something about her.*

He'd denied that it was her beauty that had caught his attention. But Charlotte kind of thought it was.

"Good afternoon, Birdie." She was suddenly self-conscious about the comfortable skirt and blouse that she'd worn to work. Not to mention her low rise, rubber-soled shoes.

As Birdie lifted her sunglasses to rest upon her head, Charlotte noticed the bruising around her eyes was still pretty colorful.

"Hi Charlotte. I was wondering if I could borrow a book."

"Of course. I've already set up that temporary library card I was talking about." She passed the card to Birdie, she smiled self-consciously.

"Thank you. It's good to have something in my pocket now. Even if it's just a library card."

"What sort of book are you looking for?"

"I'd like to read something by Dougal Lachlan. I met him at Skin Deep yesterday."

"He mentioned that."

"The two of you are dating. He told me. Plus, I heard people talking. Mostly they don't think he's good enough for you."

"Why would they think that?" God, she could feel herself blushing like a schoolgirl. How exasperating to be the talk of the local hair salon.

"Because he isn't reliable. That's what people say, anyway. But they do like his books. Belle told me she's read everything he's written. I've read them, too. I remembered that when I saw him."

"Then you know he writes true crime stories, all of them very graphic? Are you sure you want to read something like that?" She thought of her own, well-thumbed *Pride & Prejudice*. Jane Austen's civility and eloquence were always so reassuring and satisfying in times of trouble.

"I don't mind graphic stories. Plus I'm hoping reading the book will help me remember other things."

"It's probably worth a try. His books are quite popular here, obviously, but I should be able to find you one of his earlier stories."

She went to the stacks and found a copy of *A Murder In The Family*. "Would you like this one?"

"Sure."

Charlotte took back the library card, which she had set up under "Birdie Jones" and listing the emergency shelter as the address. Meanwhile, Birdie was reading "About the Author" at the back of the book.

"Says here he lives in New York City," Birdie said.

"He did. He's only recently moved back to Twisted Cedars."

"Because of you?" Birdie asked.

Damn it, she was blushing again. But before she could answer, Birdie continued.

"Or is it because he wants to write a book about those librarians who were murdered?"

Charlotte was dumbfounded.

"Belle told me there were four of them killed in the seventies. And the case might be related to a librarian here in Twisted Cedars who committed suicide right after."

"Sounds like they've been talking your ears off at that salon. Dougal was thinking about writing that story. But he's changed his mind." Or so he said.

"Too bad. It sounds like it would be interesting."

"Yes, but it's an unsolved crime and Dougal doesn't usually write about cold cases."

"He should make an exception. *Ambition should be made of sterner stuff.*"

"Isn't that from Shakespeare?" Charlotte was suddenly on alert.

Birdie looked confused. "I'm not sure where that came from."

"It came out so naturally. Maybe you're an English teacher or professor?"

Birdie looked at her hands. "I'm pretty sure I must have been a hair stylist. Maybe I read Shakespeare for pleasure?"

Right. So many people do. But Charlotte didn't voice her disbelief. She handed Birdie back her new library card.

"Thanks, Charlotte. I suppose I should return to work." She looked like she was going to leave, but then she asked, "Does it make you nervous?"

"What?"

"All those murdered librarians. And your own aunt committing suicide in this very building. It would make me nervous."

Charlotte felt as if a cold finger was tracing a line down her spine. But she forced a cheery grin. "All of that happened a long time ago."

After Birdie left, Charlotte went to make herself a cup of tea. She was upset to see her hands were trembling. Why had Birdie made such a big deal about Dougal's story? Was she just trying to distract herself from her own troubles?

Back at her desk, Charlotte did an Internet search and found the quote. It was from Shakespeare, Act Three, Scene Two, Julius Caesar.

Dougal was right. There was something about Birdie. Something very puzzling.

chapter twenty

normally the drive to Salem from Twisted Cedars would take about five hours. During RV season, when every second vehicle was pulling either a trailer or a boat, even six hours was optimistic.

Dougal didn't mind. During his years in the city, he hadn't thought much about his home state, or ever realized he missed it. Now that he was back, it seemed a love for the ocean, forest and mountains had somehow seeped into his marrow.

He played CD's from his collection—most of his music was linked to important people in his life. Right now he was listening to some piano jazz that his editor had recommended. At first listening to the dissonant harmonies was like getting a lecture, without the words.

Paula could be subtle that way. She'd grown tired of phone calls and e-mails so she'd sent him this CD.

But it was growing on him.

He stopped on the road for lunch, at a café with Wi-Fi, and set up his laptop on the table, between the plate with his club sandwich and his cup of coffee. Sometimes locating people was as simple and as low-tech as using the directory listing, and he lucked out this time. There was only one Lachlan listed in Salem and her name was Ellen.

He waited until he was finished eating, and back in the car, to call her.

When she wasn't home, he left a message explaining he was a writer doing some research and would appreciate setting up a time for an interview. He didn't tell her what the interview would be about. Didn't want to scare her off.

She returned the call while he was driving through Eugene. He took the first opportunity to pull off the highway, thinking he might need to make some notes.

"Ellen thanks for calling back. Like I said I'm—"

"Did you write *Murder In The Family*?" She wasn't interested in hearing him give his spiel again, apparently.

"I did."

"I loved that book. Are you working on another one, set here in Salem?"

"Well, I'm not sure about that. I need to do some fact-checking first."

"Don't know how I could help with that."

"That all depends on whether you knew a man by the name of Edward Lachlan. I believe his family used to own a property on the outskirts of the city about forty or fifty years ago."

There was a long silence after this. Then, "Are we related?"

"I don't know. Are we?"

"Eddie was my brother."

He noted the past tense. "Then I guess we are. Because he's my father."

* * *

Ellen suggested they meet at a Starbucks, not far off the Interstate. She said she'd recognize him from the author photograph at the back of his books.

To which he replied, "Don't be so sure about that. I've just had my hair cut."

"How different can it be?"

He conceded the point, and agreed that he could make it to the meeting place in about twenty minutes.

An attractive woman in her late sixties, with steely gray hair, was waiting for him when he arrived. He saw absolutely no resemblance to his father, but that was all explained in the first five minutes.

"We were both adopted. Our parents couldn't have biological children. I was the first. Eddie came along about four years later. My parents wanted a boy to help with the chores—we had a cherry orchard, as well as some cattle."

A piece of lint on her dark slacks seemed to catch her interest at that point. She went about carefully extracting it, then folding it up into a napkin.

Dougal waited patiently. He knew she had questions and he'd rather hear what they were than take a stab and end up saying more than he needed to.

"You write true crime books, right? Are you going to write about Eddie? I know he killed his wife—second wife, not your mother."

Dougal considered how to answer. If he admitted he had no intention of writing about this, would she still help him? "I need more facts before I decide. Have you seen him lately?"

"Haven't seen Eddie or spoken to him since the last time he ran away."

"When he was sixteen?"

She nodded.

"You said since the last time he ran away. Were there other times?"

"Oh yes. He was only six the first time he decided to leave home." Ellen sighed, and her face reflected a combination of sadness and regret that Dougal had seen on the faces of many of his interview subjects over the years.

"And he had reason to," she continued. "I don't know why, but my parents treated him really terribly. They were fine to me. But Eddie—well, I'm not sure if it was because he was a boy, or because he was so damn smart and lippy, or what it was, but they were vicious."

"Are they still in Salem?"

"Both passed on about ten years ago. We'd already sold the farm by then and they were living in a home for seniors not far from my place. I never married so I visited them almost every day.

Believe it or not, they were good parents to me. I never asked them if they regretted how they'd treated Eddie. Maybe I was afraid to hear their answers."

"What did they do to your brother?"

"You don't want to hear this."

More likely, she didn't want to re-live it. Or be judged by it. "I've interviewed a lot of people about abusive situations. It's hard. But it really helps to get the facts."

She swallowed. Turned her gaze away from him, to the window overlooking the parking lot. "They rode him hard for every bad thing he did. But it was more than that. He didn't get to sit at the table with us, he had his own place on the floor in the kitchen. We'd all get a nice meal and he'd get the scraps."

"Like a dog," Dougal said bluntly, willing himself not to feel any emotion. He'd been exposed to so much that was evil in this world. He had to pretend this was just another case, about a man he didn't really know.

Which was true in a way.

"Eddie was difficult, even as a baby. Mom and Dad liked their children to be obedient, which I guess I was. Not Eddie. Even before he was school-age, dad would take him out to the barn for whippings."

"But not you?"

"No. I was the golden child." She bit her lower lip, gnawing at it. "I was treated like a princess. I feel sick about it now."

"You were a kid. You can't blame yourself for what they did."

"I can't forget about it, either, though it hurts to remember. I guess I blame myself for not sticking up for him. If I had, he might have turned out different."

Maybe. Or maybe not. "What was he like when he got older?"

"He used to scare me. He had a real vicious streak. We had a pet cat in the house. Both my mother and I adored her. But there was a barn cat, too, a mouser. She'd run around the countryside and get pregnant every now and then. Dad always insisted we kill the kittens. That was Eddie's job and he seemed to enjoy it. He didn't put them in a sack with some rocks and drop it in the pond the way Dad suggested. He—"

"Let me guess. Did he wring their necks?"

"How did you know?"

"When I was a kid he did the same thing to my pet kitten. Shortly after that, my mother kicked him out."

"Oh, God." Ellen rubbed her face, as if she wished she could erase her wrinkles, and the past, and all those awful memories. "I wonder what might have happened to him if he'd had different parents."

Dougal thought of the way Ed had tracked down his birth mother. "I think he wondered the same thing."

But finding Shirley hadn't brought Ed any peace.

"Sometimes Eddie could be quite charming," Ellen said. "And he was smart at school. If he'd gone to college he might have had a good life."

"Maybe."

"Did he hurt you, too, when you were little?"

"No. My mother protected me. But I think she was worried that she might not be able to keep doing it. That's why she kicked him out. She was lucky to have good friends who helped her and forced him to leave town and never bother us again."

"That must be when he moved to Salem and married his second wife. The one he beat to death."

Dougal nodded. "Did you follow the case?"

"Couldn't avoid it. Eddie's trial was all over the TV and newspapers. Mom and Dad were sick about it. They discontinued their newspaper subscription, and stopped going out except for important appointments. Eddie made recluses of them. But I suppose they deserved it."

Dougal said nothing. It wasn't his job to pass judgment, but he wasn't granting absolution, either.

"Every time Ed ran away, he always said he was going to find his birth mother. I never had the heart to remind him that it was his birth mother who had given him away in the first place."

"I think he eventually figured that out. I'm pretty sure he stole his adoption records when he was twenty-two and discovered his mother was the librarian in Twisted Cedars."

"Really? Did he ever contact her?"

"I can't be sure if he did so directly. But he did send her a message, in a manner of speaking he sent four of them." Dougal told her about the murdered librarians.

Ellen's eyes grew huge. "He did that?"

"He's the one who told me about them. He was released from prison six months ago, and recently he started sending me emails, telling me about the murdered women and that he had a story for me that would be the best of my career."

"So he out-and-out admits to killing them?"

"No. But I think that's the conclusion he wanted me to draw."

Her shoulders sagged. "Those poor, innocent women. Where is Eddie now?"

"I have no idea. I caught up to him briefly in New York where I used to live. But he slipped out, just when I'd figured out who he was."

"Maybe it will be best if he stays missing."

If they could only be so lucky.

chapter twenty-one

Wednesday night Wade didn't leave the office until after nine. On his way home he did a drive-by of the women's emergency shelter. Though Birdie ought to be perfectly safe here in Twisted Cedars, he felt uneasy every time he thought about her.

If only Chet Walker had survived that crash. For his sake, and his wife's, obviously. But also so he could tell them what had caused him to veer off the road.

And what Birdie was doing in his truck.

So far all of Dunne's investigative work supported the information Mrs. Walker had provided. Chet Walker had been an honest, hardworking guy, who downloaded about two audio books a week.

None of his friends, many of them also independent truck drivers, had ever heard of him picking up a hitchhiker.

Wade eased off the accelerator as he approached the two-story emergency shelter, not intending to stop this time, just make sure all was calm and peaceful. But as his headlights swept over the grounds, a woman emerged from behind the hedge that screened the smoking area.

It was Birdie. Clearly startled, she began running for the front door. When she was almost there, she paused and looked back, shielding the glare from his headlights with a hand over her eyes.

He switched the lights off, and lowered his window. "It's me. Sheriff MacKay. Everything all right?"

Her body almost sagged with relief. "Oh. Yes. Everything is fine." She switched directions, headed toward him. "That's a lie, actually. I spaced out on a client today."

She was wearing a dress and a strappy pair of sandals. She didn't look like she belonged in Twisted Cedars. More like the streets of some big city like Seattle or Sacramento.

"What do you mean, spaced out?"

"My mind just went blank. Belle told me to take some time off. She said I was rushing things going back to work so soon. But I needed that job."

"Maybe you should check with your doctor, make sure you're okay."

"That's what Belle said. But I'm fine. I just—forgot myself for a minute, that's all." She was wringing her hands, looking past him to scan the vehicle, as if to check if anyone else was there. "Could you talk to Belle? Ask her to give me a second chance?"

"I'm with Belle on this one. A few days to rest is a good idea. You're safe here, with free shelter and food. You shouldn't feel like you need to rush to leave."

Birdie had more serious problems than finding a job. Why wasn't she this anxious about finding out who she was, and where she came from?

"How are things going with your memory? Did anything come back to you today?"

She shook her head.

"Go inside. Get some sleep. Try not to worry."

Instead, she stepped closer, reached out her hand and placed it on his arm. "Would you take me for a drive? I feel so trapped here, but I'm afraid to go for a walk on my own."

Her lovely blue eyes were focused on him beseechingly. God help him, he wanted to say yes. All his instincts were telling him she needed taking care of. But he had to be very careful not to step over any lines.

"Go inside," he repeated. "That's where you'll be safest."

She sighed. "Will I see you tomorrow?"

"I'll be working. And you should concentrate on getting better. But if you remember anything about how you came to be in that truck with Chet Walker—or what caused the accident—let me know immediately.

* * *

six days after the accident

After a restless night, Jamie decided to walk to work to clear her head. She was still wrestling with the revelation that Liz's father had known hers in prison. It seemed like everyone around her knew more about her father than she did.

Jamie turned the corner and stopped. She'd modified her route to the office so she would pass by the Quinpool home. The pretty, two-story Victorian she'd briefly shared with Kyle and his children. From this vantage point—which was on the other side of the street and down about fifty yards—she eyed the attractive clapboard, painted white with black shutters. The classic American family home.

But her wistfulness vanished when her gaze fell on the pretty porch furniture she'd bought shortly before the wedding. Kyle had been upset that she would dare make a change to the house without consulting him first. That had been one of the first signs she'd noticed that he wasn't the man she'd imagined him to be.

The yellow caution tape that had gone up after the discovery of Daisy's body was gone now, and Kyle's father's car was parked in the driveway. As she watched, the front door opened, and Jim and Kyle stepped out to the porch.

Not wanting to be seen, Jamie slipped behind the trunk of an old oak. With her head pressed hard against the rough bark, she heard Kyle's voice travel over the clear morning air.

"It won't do any good, Dad."

"It's the only way," Jim replied, his voice firm.

"You'll only make things worse. Promise me, you won't do it. I mean it Dad. You have to promise."

Jim's response was muffled. Then Jamie heard a car door open, and close.

A few seconds later, Jim drove by. Kyle wasn't with him. She counted slowly to ten, then stepped out from behind her hiding spot. Kyle must have gone inside, all was quiet again.

Jamie sprinted down the block, until she was well out of sight. The rest of the way to the office, she puzzled over what she had heard. The father and son could have been talking about anything. It may not have been relevant to her, or the investigation into Daisy's death.

But Jamie had a feeling it was.

* * *

During his drive home from Salem, Dougal's head spun with a collage of images Ellen Lachlan had planted in his head. No matter how loud he turned the music, he couldn't get the nightmare of his father's childhood out of his mind. By noon he was back at the Librarian Cottage and he'd never been so glad to see his little A-frame in the woods. Sanctuary.

First thing, even before going over his notes, he took a walk in the forest. Amid the ancient cedars, hemlocks and pines, he felt the world right itself. All that shit Ellen Lachlan had told him about might be real, but this forest was real, too. And for some damn reason, that fact comforted him.

When he came upon the spot where he'd found Daisy's body, he didn't linger. After the crime scene guys had packed up, they'd left a gaping hole. But he'd already filled it, and weeds had started to grow in the fertile soil.

It wouldn't take long for nature to reclaim this place. Never again would it be a vegetable garden, though. Daisy's death had left a permanent blight here, just as it had in the lives of her family and friends.

After his walk, Dougal had a long drink of water, then called Charlotte at the library. "I hit the bull's eye in Salem."

"You found your father's adoptive parents?" She sounded cautious, as if she was afraid to hear the answer.

"They died a while ago, but I tracked down an older sister. Ellen Lachlan."

"What was she like?"

"Ordinary, really. And surprisingly open about the kind of life my father had. It wasn't pleasant."

"I'm sorry."

"I'll tell you details when I see you. What are you and the kids up to tonight?"

"Yesterday morning they admitted they'd been getting teased by other kids about their father. They wanted to go back to Wolf Creek Camp."

"Can't blame them for that."

"Right. I called the camp director, and they had room, so I drove them up after work yesterday."

"It's a good idea to keep them out of Twisted Cedars for the next few weeks. At least until we know if Kyle is going to be charged with anything." And selfishly Dougal was glad he'd have his librarian to himself for a bit.

"Would you like to take me out for dinner tonight?" Charlotte asked, clearly thinking along similar lines.

"How about you bring Borden back here and spend the night?" Now that he was home, he simply didn't want to leave. "I can fill you in on my interview with Ellen."

"What do you think about including Jamie?" Charlotte asked. "She'll want to hear what you found out about your father."

"Might as well."

Christ. His cozy evening with the librarian was turning into a big family thing. Not his scene, at all.

* * *

"Still want to come with me to interview Jim Quinpool today?" Duane Carter asked.

The deputy was standing in the doorway to Wade's office, a to-go cup in his hands. Probably a latte. Wade felt an instant craving.

"Yup." Wade pushed away his paperwork, then got up from his desk. He was still feeling disappointed about Tuesday's interview with Muriel. He'd been almost certain the burden of her guilt would make her crack. But she'd held firm to her contention she hadn't witnessed Daisy's death. And he was holding on to his contention she was lying.

"Might want to save yourself the aggravation. Jim's less likely to turn in his son than Muriel was," Duane pointed out.

"You're probably right. But I've known Jim all my life. And I want to see his eyes when he tells me Kyle didn't lay a hand on his ex-wife." Wade fixed his hat on his head. "Where are we meeting him?"

"Quinpool Realty."

The business which Jim and Kyle owned and operated jointly had been closed since the start of the investigation, when the ID team had scoured the place for evidence. They'd found the travel records for Kyle's trips to Sacramento, which had matched up perfectly to the dates of the withdrawals from Daisy and Charlotte's joint checking account.

Wade had seen the documentation just this morning. It was good, thorough work and it would make persuasive evidence in court.

That didn't mean they couldn't use an eye witness account, or two. Just to cinch matters.

The crime scene tape had been removed, but Quinpool Realty still had a closed sign displayed in the window. When Wade tried the door, however, it wasn't locked. The reception area was uninhabited, quiet and almost dark thanks to the pulled blinds.

Wade switched on the lights, then went to the computer at the reception desk. It felt cold to the touch. The printer, and fax machine next to it, were both powered off as well.

"Jim? Are you here?"

"In my office." The voice came from behind a closed door to the left of the reception desk. Two other doors, also closed, were to the right. Presumably Kyle's office, and perhaps a storage room or kitchen.

Wade raised his eyebrows at Duane, silently questioning who should go first. Even though he outranked the deputy, this was still his deputy's investigation.

But Carter waved his hand, indicating Wade should precede him.

Sitting behind his empty desk, tall, lanky Jim Quinpool looked like a lost soul. He glanced briefly at the law men, and waved despondently toward a couple of empty chairs. "Don't know why I still come in here. Nothing to do. Haven't had a call in over a week that wasn't a client looking to get out of a contract. And Kyle is handling those."

Wade let the older man's remarks settle for a few moments. He sure wasn't going to apologize because the investigation had been bad for the Quinpools' business.

"I know this is hard, Jim. But we have some questions."

The dull light in Jim's eyes suddenly turned sharp and focused. "It's your damn questions that have caused all the problems."

"I'd say it was the illegal burial of a body that caused the problems," Duane corrected, bluntly. "Not to mention how that body happened to get dead."

"What happened that night, Jim?" Wade used a more conciliatory tone, one he imagined a priest might use, inviting a confession.

Jim tented his hands on the desk, then stared at his fingers. "She came to the house, looking to start a fight. That's what happened."

"By 'She' do you mean 'Daisy'?"

"Of course, I mean Daisy! Isn't that who you came here to talk about?"

"I just want to be clear," Wade continued. "So you, Muriel and Kyle were awake when Daisy stopped in?"

"No! Damn it, you're putting words in my mouth. Muriel was in bed, asleep, wearing her earplugs. My snoring's been getting worse as I age. She can't sleep unless she's wearing earplugs."

"But you and your son were awake?"

"We were watching TV, having a beer."

"And what about the twins?" Carter asked. He'd pulled out a notebook and was quickly scratching things down.

"They were asleep, too, of course. It was almost eleven at night."

"Pretty late for Daisy to be visiting," Wade said.

"If she was a normal person that would be true. But Daisy was sick. She claimed she was getting better, but she wasn't. She wanted shared custody of the twins, but she couldn't take care of herself, let alone a couple babies."

"How old were the twins at that time?" Carter asked.

"Almost two."

"What was Daisy wearing?" Wade asked.

The question seemed to catch Jim off guard. "I-I don't remember. Why does it matter, anyway?"

Wade sighed. "Could you just answer the question, please?"

"Even though I don't remember?"

Carter leaned in toward him. "Try."

"Fine. She was probably in jeans and a T-shirt. That's what she usually wore."

"Could you make note of that, Carter?" In fact, Daisy had been wearing strappy heels and a dress when she was buried. The dress had been made of a synthetic material that hadn't decomposed in the seven years she'd been underground.

Regular townspeople didn't dress up that often in Twisted Cedars. It seemed to Wade that Jim would have remembered if he'd seen Daisy in a dress and heels.

"Tell us as much as you can remember about what was said," Wade continued.

"Daisy started off saying she was the mother and she deserved to spend more time with her kids. Kyle asked what her doctor thought about that, and then she started swearing and getting all hysterical. Kyle offered to make her some tea, and we all went back to the kitchen. Kyle told her to be quiet so she wouldn't wake up the kids, but she just kept ranting about how unfair he was being." Jim shook his head. "As if it was Kyle's choice to have married a crazy woman."

"You and Kyle were both aware Daisy had been diagnosed with post-partum depression?" Carter asked.

"That's what that high-priced doctor the Hammond's hired in Seattle said. I didn't buy it. Daisy Hammond was a princess who couldn't handle the normal demands of being a mother." He fixed his gaze on Wade. "You remember what she was like. Her parents doted on her, they absolutely spoiled her. All she cared about was looking good and going to parties. I warned Kyle not to marry her."

"So you think the marriage was a mistake?" Duane asked.

"From the beginning," Jim concurred.

"Back to that night," Wade said. "You'd gone to the kitchen to make tea. What then?"

"Well, I put the kettle on. Kyle wanted Daisy to sit down and be quiet, but she just talked louder and louder. She was pacing around that kitchen like a caged polar bear. I could see in her eyes, her head wasn't right. I said, be quiet or leave. And that's when she pounced on me."

Jim had to stop for a moment. He cleared his throat, and then he added, "I was just defending myself, but I guess I pushed her."

Neither Wade nor Carter spoke for several seconds. Then quietly, carefully, Wade said, "Are you saying you were the one who pushed Daisy against that wall, Jim?"

With trembling hands, Jim covered his face.

At just that moment Wade heard a door open and slam closed, following by hurried footsteps. A moment later, Kyle Quinpool was at the office door. His gaze went from his father, to Wade, then back again.

"What have you done, Dad?"

chapter twenty-two

dougal had invited his sister to dinner by text, and she'd said yes, but Charlotte was the first to arrive in her vintage BMW coupe. The vehicle was so not what you'd expect a librarian to drive. She looked great behind the wheel.

And even better when she got out. She'd ditched the dull garb she usually wore at the library—why she was so determined to mold to the stereotype of a dull librarian, he couldn't fathom—and was in a pair of sexy faded jeans and a pink T-shirt. He met her in the yard and scooped her into his arms.

"I wish I could take you straight to bed. But Jamie will be here shortly."

"I know. She called me and between us we organized the menu."

"I had it covered."

"Frozen pizza doesn't cut it Dougal."

He had to smile. "It does for me."

"Again—I know." She grabbed a couple bags of groceries from the car. "Can you get Borden? She's in her carrier in the back."

"Great. I've missed the fur-ball." He knew his cat was happier in town, at Charlotte's place, but she had to get used to living out here in the forest with him.

He held her tight to his chest until they were inside, then he set her on the arm of the sofa. "Welcome home, Borden. Remember this place?"

She arched her back, so it seemed she did. When she gave him a beseeching look, he couldn't resist. So he settled on the sofa and let her claim his lap.

Meanwhile, Charlotte was in the kitchen pulling out salmon fillets, tiny potatoes and bok choy from her paper grocery bags.

"You still have wine?" she asked hopefully.

"More than a case." Last month when he'd been researching the homicide of Mari Louise Beamish from Pendleton, he'd visited Bishop Creek Winery in the Willamette Valley and come home with some excellent bottles of pinot noir.

"We're good then. Jamie's bringing a loaf of bread and dessert."

"Speaking of Jamie..." Dougal could hear another car pulling into the yard and he went out to be the welcoming committee.

Jamie held out a glass bowl of fruit salad and a baguette to him. "Make yourself useful."

They ate outside on an old wooden picnic table that had been here forever. He'd scrubbed it clean and sanded it earlier in the day.

Maybe he'd pick up some stain the next time he was in town.

The food was good, much better than frozen pizza, he had to admit.

After a first taste of everything, he told them about finding Ellen Lachlan's number in the online directory, then meeting her at a coffee shop. "Later we went to the bar, where we both had more to drink than we should have. But she had a hell of a story to tell, and I guess she had to wash it down with something that dulled the pain."

"How old is Ellen?" Jamie wanted to know.

"Four years older than Ed. So sixty-four, sixty-five. Somewhere around there."

"So she would have been very little when her parents brought our father home?"

"Yes. But she seems to remember it quite well. She said right from the beginning her parents treated Ed differently than her."

Jamie had stopped eating as soon as he began talking about Ellen. "How so?"

"They would ignore him when he was crying and leave him for hours in his dirty diapers. Ellen remembers trying to change him and her mother telling her not to bother, saying that he wasn't as special as she was."

"Why did they treat Ellen so much better than their son?" Charlotte asked. "It just doesn't make sense."

"Ellen said he was a difficult baby and he grew up to be a difficult child. Willful and stubborn, something like that."

"Lots of children are like that," Charlotte insisted. "I see them every week during reading circle."

"Well, the Lachlan's weren't equipped to handle that, I guess. From what Ellen remembers, Ed was six when he had his first beating in the barn—his father used his belt. And there were lots more. For the first two years Ellen would put salve on the welts. But when Ed turned eight, he stopped telling her about the beatings. He stopped talking to her entirely."

Jamie covered her face, as if she was trying to block the mental image he was painting. "I don't understand how anyone could do that to a child."

"I wonder if he came to hate his sister," Charlotte said. "Because she was never beaten."

"Ellen didn't come out and say so, but I think you're right. She said their mother used food to punish Edward, too. He wasn't allowed to eat the same meals as the rest of them. He was given leftovers and never dessert."

Both Jamie and Charlotte stared down at their plates. It was hard to eat good food and listen to a story like this one.

"When he was little, Ellen would sneak him food, especially ice cream which was his favorite. But that changed, as well, when he turned eight. He wouldn't accept treats of any kind from her."

"I can't bear it." Jamie looked ready to burst into tears.

"He must have been a very angry little boy." Charlotte's face was getting paler with each new detail.

He wondered if she was thinking how lucky she'd been to be adopted by a family like the Hammonds.

"Unsurprisingly, Ed tried running away a lot. When he was still talking to her, he told Ellen he was planning to find his mom. He made up elaborate stories about the house they would live in, the great food she would cook for him and the fun things they'd do together."

"Escapism like that is common in abused children," Charlotte said.

"It's just appalling that the adoption agency didn't screen his parents properly. Or that the neighbors or his teachers didn't step in to help him," Jamie said.

"Systems have improved since those days," Charlotte said. "But we still hear about too many sad cases of abuse. I don't know if society can ever eliminate it completely."

"Can you imagine how alone he must have felt?"

Jamie was fairly melting with sympathy for their old man. So next he told them about Ed being asked to drown the unwanted kittens, but choosing to wring their necks instead.

"Maybe he didn't want them to suffer," Charlotte said.

"I doubt he spared their suffering a second's concern." He'd told both his sister and Charlotte about the time his father had killed his pet kitten. He'd done it as easily as Dougal might squash a mosquito biting his arm.

"It wasn't his fault," Jamie insisted. "If he hadn't been abused..."

"Not all abused children find it so easy to kill animals."

"But he wasn't even loved as a baby," Jamie pointed out. "What chance did he have?"

Dougal didn't answer, because he didn't have one.

"What happened after he finally ran away for good?"

"The family never saw him again. Ellen said when he was arrested for killing his second wife, they didn't even talk about it, even though the case was all over the newspapers and TV."

"They didn't feel even a little bit responsible?" Jamie looked at him incredulously.

"Maybe they did. Or maybe they didn't. By then Alva Mae, Mari Louise, Bernice, Isabel, Charlotte's Aunt Shirley and Crystal Halloway were all dead. Nothing the Lachlans felt could have changed that."

There had to have been something inside Edward Lachlan, a germ of something bad that was activated by the abuse and grew into the monster that Edward became.

Dougal had been raised by a loving and kind mother.

But what if he hadn't?

Was that same seed for evil lying dormant inside him?

chapter twenty-three

day seven after the accident

the call from the Ashland Police Department came at four o'clock on Friday afternoon. The mood in the office was lighthearted, even though most of them would be on duty this weekend. Several of Wade's deputies were kidding with Marnie in the bullpen.

Wade got up to shut his office door.

"Sorry, I didn't catch that. Could you repeat?"

"I said this is Detective Todd Waverman from the Ashland Police Department."

"Right." He jotted down the name.

"We had a fellow come in fifteen minutes ago to report a missing wife and ten-month-old baby girl."

A chill washed over Wade.

"He brought pictures and the woman looks like a match to your unidentified female victim from the accident last weekend."

"Is that right?" Wade had been hoping for a break through like this. But something felt wrong.

The baby, for instance.

Not once had Birdie given any indication she might be a mother. And yes she had amnesia. But could a mother really forget something like that?

"What's the man's name?"

"Richard Caruthers. He's a director at the Shakespeare Festival we have down here. His wife works there, too, or she did before the baby was born. She did make-up and hair and acted some, too."

Checkmark to the hair and the makeup. He'd also heard her quote from Shakespeare. "Why did it take Caruthers so long to report her—them—missing?"

"He claims he left his wife and the baby last Friday at their family cabin on Hyatt Lake. That was the last he talked to her until he drove back to the cottage this morning. When he got there, her car was still parked out front, and the runabout was moored at the dock, but no one was in the cabin."

"Any signs of a break-in or struggle?"

"I'm on my way now to take a look. But Caruthers says the place seemed normal. His wife's purse was where she normally kept it, cash still in her wallet, on a hook in their bedroom. And her phone was on the kitchen table—out of juice."

"So not a robbery. Could she have gone to the neighbors?"

"Caruthers says he checked, but none of the neighbors were home. He says they didn't socialize much out there, anyway, mostly kept to themselves. I've got a crime scene team on the way. Just wanted to talk to you first."

"Our Jane Doe has remembered nothing since the accident. She still doesn't know her own name, and hasn't mentioned husband, or a baby."

Is she still in the hospital?"

"She's staying at the Heartland Women's Shelter here in Twisted Cedars. She came to us all bruised up—looked like she'd been handled pretty roughly in the weeks before the accident."

"That's interesting. Think the husband roughed her up?"

"It's one explanation." He was out of his chair. Pacing. Thinking. "What's your take on the husband?"

"Seemed genuinely upset—especially about his kid. Though I take that with a grain of salt. Not just because he's the husband and I'm not going to take his word as gospel—but he works in theatre for God's sake. If he needed to act upset about a missing wife and kid, I guess he could."

"Saying he roughed up his wife—what do you suppose happened to the kid?"

"God only knows."

Wade sketched out a possible scenario. Suppose there'd been a terrible fight between this Richard Caruthers and Birdie. Caruthers does something to hurt their child. Maybe even killed him. Birdie might have been so terrified, she ran, eluding her husband until she made it up to the highway. Maybe she stayed hidden for a while.

Then Chet Walker's truck appears in the distance. She leaves her safe spot and waves him down.

But why doesn't she ask Walker to call 911?

Unless she was in such a state of shock she couldn't talk. Walker can see she needs help. Probably offers to take her to the police, or a hospital.

Instead, she pulls out that piece of paper she'd ripped out of the back of Dougal's book, where she'd underlined *Twisted Cedars*.

Why she would want to go to Dougal Lachlan's birthplace, Wade had no idea. But this scenario would explain why Chet Walker hadn't driven his usual route to Port Orford, but instead had taken the more treacherous mountain road to their town.

Wade didn't share any of his speculations with Waverman. At this point they had better focus on facts.

"How far is the Caruthers' cottage from the Interstate?"

"About five miles to the 66." The detective gave him the coordinates for the cottage, and Wade went to the map of Oregon on his wall. Taking a red pin, he marked the location.

"And do the Caruthers have a house in Ashland?"

"Yup. Just sent an officer over there, too. With Caruthers' permission she's going to give the place an initial search. Think you could get one of your men to interview your Jane Doe on our behalf? Maybe if you mention her husband and baby, she'll start to remember."

The puzzle pieces of Birdie's life were coming together fast and furious.

Birdie... He shouldn't think of her that way anymore.

"What's her name? The missing wife?"

"Hang on." There was the sound of papers being shuffled. Then, "The daughter is Josephine. The woman—Joelle Caruthers."

* * *

Wade had heard of the Ashland Shakespeare Festival, though he'd never been. A few times his Mom had taken trips with a group of women from town, though. She'd raved about it.

He found the official website for the Oregon Shakespeare Festival, and froze at the sight of the logo. It was the capital letter "O" with a short dash on the top left corner.

Birdie's tattoo.

In his mind this cleared away any doubts that the woman the Ashland police were looking for was Birdie. But still he clicked on "OSF Company" and from there searched through the list of artists until he found a picture and biography for Richard Caruthers. The man had lots of thick, dark hair and might have been good looking except for an overly generous chin.

The attached biography had no personal details, other than listing his educational background which comprised a BA from the University of Michigan and an MA from Northwestern. Richard had been with the OSF for twelve seasons, the first eight as assistant director, and now as director. He was currently involved in a production of Henry V.

With a bit more trepidation, Wade looked up Joelle Caruthers. He found her listed in two places. In the Production Department under wigs and makeup, and also as an actor, where her credits included being the understudy for Biondello in The Taming of the Shrew and Cordelia in King Lear.

For a long time he stared at her photo.

There was no doubt this woman was Birdie. But there was also something fundamentally different between the photograph as she'd been then and the woman who'd survived that truck accident.

This Joelle Caruthers was confident, beautiful, with a hint of the siren in the gleam of her eyes. She was obviously focused directly on the camera. But Birdie, as she was now, rarely looked anyone in the eye. She was perpetually distracted by something in the distance, or off to the side.

Or, perhaps, back in her past?

* * *

Wade filled Duane in on the update, but when his deputy offered to interview Birdie, told him he'd handle it. "She's still emotionally fragile. And at least she knows me."

As Wade drove to the women's shelter, the clouds that had been building since last night finally began expelling a fine mist. He turned his wipers on at their slowest speed and they'd only managed to sweep across the windshield about ten times before he arrived at his destination.

Four children, with a watchful mother, were on the playground to the left of the building. To the right, a group of six women were smoking and casting worried looks upward.

Birdie—Joelle—wasn't in either place.

Inside, Wade checked in at the front desk. A few minutes later, Birdie—Joelle—came to the reception area, looking relieved to see him.

"I have a bad feeling about this rain," she said, clutching his arm.

"It won't last long. Rain in July is rare."

She didn't look reassured.

"We need to talk," he said. "Someplace private."

She studied his eyes, as if trying to get a hint of what was to come. When he remained quiet she said softly, "We can talk in my room."

Wade followed her down the hall, then up the stairs. Her room had very little in it. One of Dougal Lachlan's books was on the bedside table, turned so he could see the author photo, but not the title.

"Have you ever met him? Dougal Lachlan."

She nodded. "I shampooed his hair a few days ago."

"I mean before that. Before the accident."

When she shrugged helplessly, he had to remind himself to be patient with her. Just because they'd found out who she was, didn't mean she knew any more about her past now, than she had the last time he spoke to her.

All he could do was hope Waverman was right. That when he told her what he knew, her memory would be tweaked.

"We should sit down," he said.

Birdie waved him toward the only chair—wooden, with a spindle back—then perched on the edge of her neatly made bed.

"Is it bad news?" she finally asked.

He realized he'd been quiet for a long time. "Has anything come back to you, yet? Your name? Where you came from?"

"No." Her expression changed from trepidatious to fearful. "Have you heard something? Did someone from my past finally come looking for me?"

"You have a husband, and he called the Ashland police department today to report that you were missing."

With trembling fingers, Birdie—Joelle—tucked her hair behind her ears, revealing a flash of her tattoo.

He pointed to it. "That symbol on your arm. It's the logo for the Shakespeare Festival in Ashland."

She cupped her hand protectively over the tat, and nodded. "Shakespeare. Yes, that sounds right. These lines have been popping into my head. They were old English, and seemed so bizarre. But of course, they were lines from a play." She blinked. "So I wasn't a hair stylist, after all? I was an actor...?"

So she was still not remembering. Or, he forced himself to consider, still pretending not to remember.

"You were both. You did hair and makeup for productions and you were also an understudy for a couple of plays."

"And my name—?"

"Joelle Caruthers. Your husband is Richard." He'd paused to see if the names would jolt her brain into remembering.

But she only blinked. "Joelle," she repeated softly. "Joelle Caruthers. It's a pretty name. But I don't think it's me."

"There's a picture of you on the OSF Company website. You look exactly like Joelle Caruthers."

"But—I don't think I'm married."

His gaze went to the pale line on the finger on her left hand. "Looks like until very recently you wore a ring on that finger."

She rubbed at the tan line, as if she could make it disappear. "I don't like this," she said.

"There's one more thing, Joelle," he said, deliberating using her name. "According to the missing person's report filed by Richard Caruthers, the two of you had a baby. A ten-month-old girl named Josephine. She's missing too."

Joelle's face had turned very pale. But she didn't say a word.

"According to your husband, he left the two of you alone at your cottage on Hyatt Lake last Friday. I'm going to need you to come with me and give your statement."

Wade felt like a jerk, as Joelle just sat there looking shell-shocked.

He tried a gentler tone. "Do you remember Josephine?"

Slowly her eyes filled with tears. Eventually she got up and pulled something from under her pillow. Then she turned and handed him the yellow flannel blanket that had been in the truck when it crashed.

He accepted the blanket, remembering how he'd used it to stench her wound. The blood was gone. It smelled of fabric softener.

"How did you get this?"

"One of the nurses told me it came in with me when I was admitted. She asked if I wanted to keep it. And I did."

"Where is your baby, Joelle?" He handed the blanket back to her and she pressed the soft fabric to her check.

"I don't know."

chapter twenty-four

eight days after the accident

Wade had arranged with Duane, to drive to the Caruthers' cottage on Hyatt Lake early the next morning. Wade made a stop outside the Buttermilk Café so his deputy could pick up sandwiches and coffees for the drive, and Duane came back with a veggie wrap for himself, cheddar and beef for Wade, as well as two to-go cups.

"Forgot you like your coffee black, and I asked for two lattes," Carter apologized as he filled the cup holders. "Want me to run back and change the order?"

"Don't bother. This is fine." As Wade took a sip of the rich, creamy latte, he wondered if his deputy was on to him. One day he might have to publically admit he preferred these things.

They arrived at the Caruthers' cottage just before two in the afternoon. The log building was nestled into a grove of aspen and the short driveway was so jammed with emergency response vehicles they had to pull in on the shoulder of the main road. Parked near the house was a cherry red Mazda, which Wade assumed to be Joelle's vehicle.

He stopped to glance in the window and felt his chest tighten at the sight of a baby's car seat in the rear. A take-out cup from Starbucks was in the cup-holder, but apart from that, the interior was neat.

As he straightened, one of the officers from Ashland, a tall, blond man, obviously the one in charge, approached him.

"I'm Wade MacKay." He showed his badge, then introduced his deputy.

"You made good time. Todd Waverman." The tall blond man offered him a hand. Todd looked to be in his fifties. He had rough features and a no-bull-shit manner about him. "The baby is still missing. We've contacted the usual babysitter, but the husband already spoke to her and she has no clue. As for the husband, he's still being questioned up in Ashland. Have you spoken to Joelle?"

"We got her statement, but it's not helpful. She didn't recognize her name when I told her who she was. She has no memory of her husband or baby either—though the fact that she had worked for the Shakespeare Company seemed familiar to her. According to the neurologist who treated her after the accident, unpredictable memory loss is not uncommon with the sort of severe head injury she sustained in the accident."

"That could be." Waverman's eyes narrowed in the bright sunlight. "Or she feels guilty about something and she's faking amnesia."

Wade pushed aside an unexpected—and inappropriate—urge to protect Joelle. "That's possible, of course."

"Has your team found anything in the cottage?" Duane asked. He had out his pen and notebook and had been busy jotting things down since they arrived.

Wade gave the cottage another look. It was an attractive place, but small. At best it would have two bedrooms.

"No sign of a struggle, no traces of blood. Nothing. We found her purse and her phone right where her husband said they would be. We've also recovered her laptop and we've got someone going through her recent calls and emails. Top priority is searching the grounds—there's a lot to cover. The cottage comes with about five acres of land, stretching back to the lake."

Wade followed the line of Todd's finger. The lake wasn't far, maybe three hundred feet from the home. A sandy path cut through the woods toward it. About seven or eight suited-up searchers were visible from where he stood. He imagined more were fanned out over the property.

"Mind if we take a quick look inside?"

"Suit up, then go on in. It's a peculiar case. If you see anything we missed, let me know."

Wade stepped inside, feeling more curious than normal about a potential crime scene. Homes revealed a lot about the people who lived there. And he knew so little about Joelle and who she'd been before the accident.

Hopefully he'd fill in some of the empty blanks here.

The air inside was stale, at odds with the cheery pale-green paint and bright-red fabric on the sofa and chairs. Sandals and running shoes were piled by the door and several colorful baby toys were strewn on the living room carpet. Other than that, the entry and living room looked neat.

Wade passed through an arched opening to the kitchen, which had pine cabinetry and white appliances. A high-chair was parked next to the table and several plastic bowls and bottles had been left on a rack to dry by the sink.

On the fridge were about a dozen photographs, most of them of a baby girl, from infancy to what Wade presumed was close to her current age of ten months.

Cute kid.

But what really drew his interest were the three photographs of Joelle and Richard Caruthers. One had been taken on a beach, another at a restaurant and a third on stage. In the third photo, Joelle was wearing a period costume and Richard was dressed in black jeans and shirt. He appeared to be giving her instruction about something.

Duane stuck close behind him as he gave the rest of the cottage a quick tour. There were other framed photos in the bedroom projecting the same image of a happy couple and their new child. Two nightstands flanked the queen-sized bed. One was tidy, with only a lamp and a small bowl containing change.

The other had a bottle of hand cream, a half-empty glass of water, a pair of pink reading glasses and a book that gave Wade a sense of *déjà vu*. It was one of Dougal's, *A Murder in the Family*. With gloved hands, Wade picked it up and turned it over.

He was pretty sure this was the same book he'd seen in Joelle's room in the women's shelter. As he flipped through the pages, the story came back to him. It was about a man who'd killed his wife and gotten away with it for fifteen years before the cops finally built a case against him.

When he flipped all the way to the back, he saw a page had been ripped out. No doubt this was the author bio page he'd found in Chet Walker's truck.

He pointed out the find to Duane, who made a note of it, then took the book to one of Todd Waverman's team members to be filed as evidence.

Meanwhile Wade moved on to the bathroom. There were several baskets containing an astonishing large number of beauty projects. He supposed that made sense given that Joelle had done hair and makeup for a living.

To the right of the bathroom was a tiny second bedroom with only space enough for a crib, small dresser and a rocking chair. The color scheme was white and yellow, which reminded Wade of the flannel blanket Joelle had been carrying with her in the truck. He'd included the detail in Joelle's statement. It might prove important at some point.

On his way down the back hall, Wade turned for a final look at the main living area. The afternoon sun was coming in the south-facing windows, and something glinted in a narrow space between the pine floorboards.

He went to investigate, and plucked out a delicate wedding band. There was an inscription in letters so tiny Wade could hardly read them: *Never Doubt My Love*, followed by a year, which Wade assumed was when Joelle and Richard had married. As he passed this to another of the crime scene people, he wished he could take it back to Twisted Cedars, and like Cinderella's prince with the slipper, try it on Joelle's finger.

He had no doubt that it would fit.

But why was it here, on the floor? Had it fallen accidentally, somehow? Or had Joelle flung it at Richard in a rage during an argument?

chapter twenty-five

as Wade and his deputy exited through the back of the cottage, a robin inspecting the grass for worms flew up into a nearby fir tree for cover. Wade and Carter followed the path to the lake. There was a fire pit at the halfway point, circled by four Adirondack chairs. Five officers were searching the shoreline and Todd Waverman was one of them. When he spotted Wade, he scrambled up the bank, and motioned that they should sit on the chairs by the fire pit.

"What did you think of the cabin?" Todd asked.

Wade told him about the book and the wedding ring. "Seems odd she would come to Twisted Cedars because she saw the name in a bio at the end of a book. Doesn't make sense. As for the wedding ring, you can tell Joelle used to wear one. She has a tan line. So I'm pretty sure it's hers."

"Sounds reasonable," Todd agreed.

Deputy Carter looked up from taking his notes. "You stated Richard Caruthers left his wife and kid behind on Friday and that was the last time he spoke to her. Did he talk to them by phone at any time in the week?"

"He claims he was too busy with work. Apparently opening night for the play is next week."

"That sounds fishy to me, sir," Duane said. "My wife and I don't even have a kid, but if I left her for a week, she'd want me to phone. No matter how busy I was."

Wade nodded, mulling over the timeline. "When did Caruthers say he left the cottage on Friday night?"

"After dinner, around eight o'clock." One of the men at the lake called out, and Todd jumped to his feet. Wade and Carter followed him down to the shore. But when the man who'd called the alert, withdrew his net from the lake, all he had was an old hiking boot.

Todd shook his head, discouraged, then refocused on their conversation. "Where were we? Oh, yeah. Caruthers. He says he drove directly home that Friday night, and stayed there, but he has no witnesses."

"Maybe he spent some time on the home computer?"

"Nope. Says he just watched TV then went to bed."

So it would be impossible to verify his story.

"If the husband is telling the truth, something happened to Joelle and the baby between that time, and a week later when he showed up at the cottage on Friday morning," Wade said.

"Agreed. So let's come at this from the other side," Todd suggested. "What time did that truck driver leave Klamath Falls a week later on Saturday morning?"

"Seven a.m." Carter had flipped back a few pages in his notebook. "Which would put Chet Walker in the right section of highway 66 around eight a.m."

"Fastest I could imagine Joelle walking the five miles from the cottage to the 66 is about two hours," Wade said. "Longer if she was injured, or disoriented."

"So something happened between eight o'clock Friday night and six the following morning." The Ashland Detective shook his head. "That's a big spread of time. We'll get more people out questioning the neighbors. But so far no one has come forward as having heard or seen anything out of the ordinary in the past two weeks."

"Have you checked with their neighbors in town?" the deputy asked. "To see if they can confirm the husband's arrival home on Friday?"

"We're in the process of checking. So far, no luck confirming the Friday night alibi. But the closest neighbors on either side have admitted to hearing arguments at the Caruthers' home since the baby was born."

"And what does the husband have to say about that?" Wade wondered.

"He admits the baby not sleeping well has caused some stress. Joelle wishes he would spend more time at home, helping her. But he's getting pressure from the Theatre, too, needing this next play to be a big success."

"Nothing too out of the normal, there," Duane said.

"We've just started our investigation," Waverman said. "I suspect more dirt will rise to the surface."

Wade didn't doubt that it would.

* * *

When they were ready to leave, Wade asked if he could take one of the photos of Joelle with her husband, and another of Josephine. "The pictures might help Joelle remember."

Todd agreed it was worth a try. He'd no sooner asked one of his men to seal the two photos in plastic, than his attention was caught by a new vehicle pulling to a stop on the road.

Wade looked as well. A C model, black Mercedes was pulling up behind Wade's SUV, and a well-dressed man wearing sunglasses stepped out. He was medium height, with a barrel chest and long legs. Even from a distance, Wade immediately recognized him from the photos as Richard Caruthers. The chin gave him away.

Todd wasn't happy. "He ought to know better than to be here. I warned him this morning we were cordoning off the area."

"We'll remind him on our way out," Wade offered. He asked Duane to wait for the photographs, then made his way down the lane and to the road.

Caruthers was looking at Wade's SUV, and as Wade approached, the other man lifted his sunglasses and narrowed his eyes. "Why are the authorities from Curry County here? Is that where my wife is? Have you found my daughter?"

"No news on your child, I'm afraid."

The man's shoulders sagged.

Wade introduced himself. "And you, I presume, are Richard Caruthers."

Without leaving time for the other man to confirm this fact, he continued, "Detective Waverman has a message for you. He'd like you to return home and keep yourself available for further questioning."

"If your wife had been in an accident and been gone for a week, and your child were missing, would you be okay with sitting at home by a phone and waiting for news?"

Wade studied the man, wishing his true motivations could be read as easily as the designer name on the side of his sunglasses. Was he an innocent man, distraught about his wife and missing daughter?

Or did he know a lot more than he was telling?

Wade kept his tone neutral. "It's not easy. But you're better off leaving this to the professionals. I've seen many a search effort bungled by a well-meaning, but untrained civilian."

"They told me my wife has been found. That she was in a truck accident last Saturday—"

The man's voice broke, and he couldn't go on. He went back to his car and pulled out a bottle of water. After a long drink he asked, "Is she okay? They told me she had a brain injury."

The Ashland police would have answered these questions for him. But Wade could understand a man needing to hear it twice. "She's been released from the hospital, but she has some memory issues. In fact, she doesn't know her own name. She doesn't remember you, either."

"Our baby?"

"No."

"I can't believe this. It's like a god-dammed horror movie. Can't you at least tell me where Joelle is? I have to see her."

"Probably not a good idea just yet,"

Duane joined them then. As he introduced himself to Caruthers, he tucked the photos into his jacket pocket.

Wade watched as his deputy made a head to toe sweep of the man.

"Nice socks," he commented.

"What?" Caruthers looked from the deputy, to his own legs. Pulling up on his dark, tailored jeans he revealed socks that matched the violet shade of his shirt. "Who the hell cares about my socks?"

"Well, you do, I guess. Since you took the time to color coordinate your outfit. Nice shoes, too. Italian?"

Caruthers looked at him as if he was nuts. "How can it matter where I bought my shoes?"

"Just think it's funny. If I was going to a cottage for a summer weekend, I'd probably wear sandals, shorts and a T-shirt. But hey. That's me."

Caruthers was clearly flustered by Carter's observations. "I didn't know my child was missing when I got dressed this morning. And I sure as hell didn't realize my wife was in a crash last Saturday and that she doesn't even remember who she is anymore."

"I guess if you'd called her some time during the week, though, we would have found out these things sooner."

"I was busy. And we'd had an argument. I figured she needed time to cool off." Caruthers' shoulders slumped. "You're right, though. I should have called. I should have checked on her. Joelle always says I get too obsessed about my work. I wish to God—"

But he didn't share what he was wishing, instead he began to pace alongside his car, his fine leather soles crunching on the gravel.

"I haven't got a clue what to do right now. Sitting and waiting at home is impossible."

"Do you have family you can call?"

He pulled his phone out of his pocket, started scrolling. "My parents are in a care home. Neither one is very healthy. I'm not going to upset them until I know for sure what's going on. Joelle's mom died a long time ago. I do have a sister in Chicago. But she has three kids and a job..." He pocketed the phone.

"Friends?" Carter suggested.

"All of my friends are at the theatre. Christ. The play. We're supposed to open in six days." He sagged against the side of his car.

"As always, Shakespeare says it best. When sorrows come, they come not single spies but in battalions." He stopped. "That probably sounds pretentious to you. But whatever's happened in my life—both the good and the bad—Shakespeare has always had the perfect words to describe what I'm feeling."

Wade exchanged a glance with Duane, and could tell they were both thinking the same thing. If Caruthers was in the mood to talk, they sure as hell were going to stick around and listen.

"You said there'd been an argument. What was it about?"

"What do all couples with a young child argue about? She thought I was working too much. And she was right. We hadn't planned on having children. The theatre—and Joelle. That was all I needed to make me happy."

"So life was pretty much perfect...before the baby came along?" Wade prompted.

"Yes. And no. The reality of a baby is different than the perception. Of course I fell in love with her the moment she was born. I keep thinking about her. How cute she looked in her new Winnie-the-Pooh pajamas, the last time I saw her. She loved when I read those stories to her."

"Loved?" Wade's eyebrows shot up at Caruthers' use of the past tense. "Do you think your daughter is dead, Richard?"

"I don't know what to think. But I'm scared. Wouldn't you be?" Caruthers was gazing down at the lake now, where a couple divers were suiting up at the end of the dock.

"You keep looking toward the lake. Did your daughter like the water?"

"She was scared of it. But she was only ten months old. Still in the crawling stage." Caruthers wheeled on Wade, suddenly. "You have to let me talk to Joelle. I need to know what happened."

"Calm down." Wade put a hand on the man's chest and forced him to take a few steps backward.

"Can you tell me about Joelle's accident, at least? Detective Waverman said she was in a truck that drove off the road and down an embankment. I looked it up online. The stories say the driver died. His name was Chet Walker and he was forty-six years old. What was my wife doing in his truck in the first place?"

"Maybe you can help us with that. Had Joelle ever hitchhiked before, to your knowledge?"

"Of course not. No one does that anymore."

"She must have been pretty desperate."

"I've been trying to make sense of it. Maybe a stranger broke into the cottage. Attacked her and Josephine. Maybe he took Josephine away and Joelle was running for help. It's the only thing that makes sense."

"I wonder if that stranger also gave Joelle a beating a week earlier?" Wade inserted the question casually, but Caruthers immediately went on the alert.

"Why do you say that?"

"Just trying to understand why Joelle's body was covered in bruises when we found her. Bruises that hadn't been caused by the accident because they were at least a week old."

That shut Caruthers up. But only for a few moments.

"They probably happened in her self-defense class. She told me one of the participants got a little carried away at their last session."

"Self-defense class?"

"Didn't Joelle tell you? Doesn't she remember anything?"

"Not much," Wade said.

"Well, she was worried about spending so much time alone out here with the baby. Last thing we need is a dog so she signed up for self-defense classes. She had her last session the night before she and the baby came out here."

chapter twenty-six

It was four-thirty when Wade and Carter finally convinced Richard Caruthers to leave the cottage and go home.

They followed behind him all the way to Ashland and a small, Tudor-styled house with rose bushes in the front. A van and a squad car were parked out front, and the property had been cordoned off with yellow tape.

Seemed like Caruthers couldn't go home now, either.

Wade checked in with the crime scene techs, while Caruthers was escorted upstairs to pack a suitcase.

Every hour the baby remained missing, chances of finding her alive grew smaller. Wade was afraid that already it was too late.

Two men were examining the back yard carefully. The contents of the trash can and compost bin had been emptied onto tarps, and would undoubtedly be sifted carefully for evidence.

Fifteen minutes after he'd arrived, Richard Caruthers had his suitcase packed and was ready to leave.

"Where will you go?" Wade asked him.

"To the theatre. Where else?"

Once they'd watched him drive off, Wade asked Duane if he wanted to grab a meal before they drove back to Twisted Cedars.

"Why not. Maybe we should pick up some tickets and take in a show after. Seems a shame to be right here and not go to a play," Duane was on his phone, looking up something. "I bet we could get tickets to *Much Ado About Nothing*. Play starts in just two hours."

Wade couldn't imagine anything he'd rather not do. "That's Shakespeare, right?"

"One of his romantic comedies. I bet you'd love it."

"Oh, probably. But what would your wife think?"

"Good point. She'd be upset if I saw it without her. Sorry I shouldn't have said anything. Probably got your hopes up."

Wade gave his deputy an incredulous glance and Duane laughed.

* * *

Charlotte was aware that the administrators at Wolf Creek Camp didn't encourage parents or guardians to phone their children during their time away. Their reasoning was that often children who were having fun before the call, would end up homesick after. But in Cory and Chester's case, they had agreed to make an exception.

So Friday afternoon, during a quiet moment at work, Charlotte called to see how they were settling. Chester was on the line, first.

"I'm fine," was all he said when she asked how he was.

"Are you having fun?"

"Yup."

"No problems with the other kids?"

"Nope."

Charlotte sighed. "You know that if you and your sister aren't happy, I can be there in two hours to pick you up."

"We're good."

"Okay. Well, I'm glad you're having fun. Let me talk to your sister."

Cory chattered on about the horse rides and the big bonfire they'd had the previous evening. Just as Charlotte was about to say goodbye, though, she did admit that the news about their Mom had spread throughout the camp.

"No one is being mean, but they look at us as if we're weird."

"Do you want to come home?"

"No. We're okay."

The twins were not going to be able to outrun this, no matter where they went. Not unless she moved them at least a thousand miles away, and even then, the scandal might follow, thanks to the Internet and social media.

She'd have to help them learn to cope. The only way to deal with the gossip and innuendo was to face it.

Not that she'd ever done that in her own life. Maybe she and the kids would have to learn together.

She'd been adopted into the Hammond family to be a companion to Daisy, and her parents had been nothing but kind to her. Yet they'd fostered an illusion that they were a perfect, happy family, when the truth was Daisy had disliked and resented her from the beginning to the end. The family albums were filled with pictures of the two of them, posed together with pretty smiles. No one would guess Daisy was pinching Charlotte's shoulder, or that she'd just kicked her in the shin.

If they had been open about the conflict, instead of denying it, would she and Daisy have had a better relationship? She would never know the answer to that.

At quarter to five Birdie entered the library looking lost.

No. Not Birdie.

Terri Morrison from Heartland had called Charlotte today and told her Birdie was really Joelle Caruthers from Ashland. Apparently she had a husband—and a ten-month old baby who was currently missing.

Joelle still remembered none of this.

And from the looks of her, she was still walking around in a fog of forgetfulness.

Charlotte got out of her chair. "May I help you, Joelle?"

"I-I don't know. I think I need to talk to Dougal Lachlan..."

"He lives about five miles out of town," Charlotte explained, wondering why in the world Joelle should need to talk to Dougal.

"I heard he sometimes works here. You know, writing his books."

"Sorry but he isn't here right now."

"I just have this feeling that I need to talk to him. I can't even say why. I guess that sounds strange."

Charlotte felt sorry for her. She'd been in a car crash. Now her baby was missing—possibly dead. But it was weird the way she seemed fixated on Dougal.

"He's out at his cabin. It's too far to walk to."

"I've heard about that place. When I was cutting her hair, the mayor's wife said people around town call it the Librarian Cottage because your aunt used to live there."

"That's true."

"That's the aunt who killed herself, right? Here, in the basement?"

It had been unconscionable for Belle and her stylists to fill Joelle's head with all these stories. Didn't they realize how vulnerable she was?

"That was a very long time ago."

Joelle's eyes flickered. "The Sheriff came to talk to me. He told me I have a baby. But that can't be right. I don't think I'm this Joelle Caruthers person. Do you?"

Charlotte didn't know how to answer her. "It's almost closing time. How about I lock things up here and give you a ride back to the shelter?"

She would have to call Wade later, and tell him about this. It seemed to her that Joelle was getting worse, not better.

* * *

Jamie left work early on Friday afternoon, to meet a realtor at a house on Horizon Hill Road. She'd been surfing the web during her lunch hour and spotted the two bedroom bungalow, neat and fairly new, built on a hill. On a whim, she'd contacted the realtor, who had set up a viewing right away.

The misty rain of the morning had left only wispy clouds behind, so Jamie was able to appreciate the stunning view of the ocean from the street. She guessed the view would be even more amazing inside.

The realtor was waiting for her at the front door. Bailey Landax was in her mid-forties, a polished blonde who looked as if her hair had been lacquered and her makeup layered to withstand anything the weather on the Oregon Coast could throw at it.

She had fashionable sling-back shoes, a Michael Kors purse and a Kate Spade wrap-around dress. "Jamie! So nice to meet you! You'll love this house. A real charmer. I listed it just last week."

As Bailey led her on a tour, Jamie felt oddly removed, almost like she was watching a reality TV show, not actually here in person listening as the realtor pointed out all the best features. The well-appointed bathrooms and kitchen. The large, walk-in closet. The cozy fireplace in the family room.

"Very nice." Jamie could sense Bailey had hoped for more enthusiasm.

"If you're looking for something larger, I have several other listings I could show you."

"This has more than enough space for me." In fact it felt palatial compared to her old double-wide. Jamie wasn't sure she could handle having so much space, living on her own. Kyle's house had been massive by her standards, too, but at least she'd shared that one with a husband and two kids.

Unwanted tears blurred her vision, and, afraid she was going to break down on the spot, she made up a pressing appointment and promised Bailey she'd be in touch real soon.

Once in her car, Jamie drove down the hill, pulled into a side street, then parked, and wept.

She cried for everything she'd lost the last two years. Her mother. The home where she'd grown up. Her marriage and her happily-ever-after dreams.

Fifteen minutes later, she was drying the tears and chiding herself for her breakdown, when a text message came through.

I'VE SEEN YOU COME BY MY HOUSE. I KNOW YOU MISS ME TOO. CAN WE MEET?

Oh Kyle. He'd always had a gift for catching her at her weakest.

NO POINT, she replied. But even as she typed out the words, she knew she was going to go.

* * *

Kyle had an open bottle of wine and some cheese and crackers on the kitchen island. Despite the stress lines around his eyes and mouth, he still looked handsome, dressed in slim fitting pants and a shirt the same shade of blue as his eyes.

But Jamie's gaze kept being pulled to the corner wall, where she guessed Daisy had cracked her head.

If Kyle noticed her fascination with the spot, he pretended not to. Instead he poured her a glass of the same pinot noir they'd ordered for their wedding.

Jamie perched tentatively on a stool and took a sip. Kyle, on the other side of the kitchen watched her.

"I shouldn't have driven by your house last night," Jamie said. "I'm sorry if it gave you the wrong impression."

"What would the right impression be?"

"That I'm having a hard time believing what a bad decision I made."

"You mean by marrying me."

She gave him a "Duh," look.

"Look, Jamie, I admit I lied to you. But I did it for my kids, wanting to protect them. I see now that it was stupid. Not only have I lost them, but you as well."

She sighed. "What's done, is done."

"But if you gave me a second chance, I promise things would be different. I have learned from my mistakes."

"You sound sincere. I'm sure, right now, you believe what you're saying."

"Is it so inconceivable that a man can change?"

She didn't answer.

"I can. And I will." He turned to look at the photos that covered his fridge. "I miss them so much."

"I'm sure they miss you, too."

She could see him swallow hard. He was fighting back tears, and she didn't believe it was an act.

"They shouldn't be living with Charlotte. They hardly know her." Kyle placed his hands on the island and leaned in toward her. "You should petition the court for custody. Cory and Chester love you. If they can't be with me, they should be with you."

"What?" She hadn't seen the request coming, yet she had to admit she'd entertained the idea herself. She had even gone so far as to discuss the matter with her lawyer. "The courts favor biological relatives. You and I weren't married for even two months."

"But we dated for six months before we got married. And you saw them nearly every day. They were lucky if they spent two days a year with their Aunt Charlotte."

And wasn't that Kyle's fault? Charlotte had told her that Kyle made it difficult for her to see Daisy's children.

Jamie nibbled at the cheese tray, but the camembert was cold and the crackers broken.

It wasn't in her nature to question Kyle's motives, but in this case she'd be a fool not to. All this talk about wanting a second chance was bogus. He hadn't really loved her. Ever.

He'd married her because he needed someone to run his household and look after his kids. Now he probably wanted her to have custody of the twins because he figured he could control her better than he could Charlotte.

"It doesn't make sense for me to request custody of Chester and Cory." She set down her wine glass. "Not when I'm seeing my lawyer next week about an annulment."

chapter twenty-seven

Joelle looked distraught, on the verge of panicked, when Wade picked her up on Saturday morning outside the women's shelter. It was dawn, and a beautiful peacefulness hung over the town. But Joelle was impervious to the beauty of the sunrise, or the sweet smell of the air. She'd been calling the office repeatedly for the past fifteen minutes saying she needed to speak to the Sheriff. No one else would do.

Usually Joelle took pains with her grooming, probably out of habit, more than an attempt to impress anyone in Twisted Cedars. But this morning her hair was uncombed and she wore no makeup. She was dressed in faded-looking grey sweatpants and a blue T-shirt.

She said hello without looking at him, fumbled with her seat belt until he reached over and fastened it for her.

"What's wrong?"

"I had an awful dream last night. About the accident. Except it wasn't a dream. It was real." Tears were pooled in her eyes when she turned to him.

"That's good. It means you're starting to remember."

"What if I don't want to remember?"

He'd been planning to take her to the office, but she looked so weak and shaken. "When's the last time you ate?"

"Last night."

"What exactly?"

It took her a while to recall. "Yogurt and an apple."

"How about we go for a cup of herbal tea and a muffin while we talk?" He didn't think coffee would be a good idea. She seemed jumpy enough already.

He drove to Frosty's Donuts, a favorite of both truckers and cops since it was open twenty-four seven. They sat in a corner booth and placed orders with a teenaged boy with tats running up both arms from his wrists to the short sleeves of his black T-shirt.

"I'll have a coffee and a maple bacon donut," Wade said.

Joelle wrinkled her nose.

"Better than it sounds," he assured her.

"Green tea and a pumpkin muffin for me, please."

After their server left, Wade focused on Joelle. "What did you remember?"

"In my dream I was in a truck with a strange man. We were driving on windy mountain roads that were making me carsick." Her eyes darted from him, to the table top, then to the view out the window.

Wade didn't take his eyes off her face.

"Then I sat up in bed. I was awake. I touched my cheeks to make sure. But the dream didn't stop, because it wasn't a dream. I was remembering. "

His gut clenched so tight he couldn't have handled even a sip from the glass of water in front of him. Sensing it would be a mistake to push, he waited for her to continue.

"The man in the truck—he was Chet Walker. He was chewing gum. Peppermint. He offered me some and I said no."

Wade recalled seeing the blue package in the wreckage after the crash.

"He was talking. He'd been talking for a long time. I remember wishing he would just be quiet and let me rest."

"Can you recall him picking you up? Where you were? Why you were hitchhiking?"

"No. It starts in the truck. I have nothing before then."

"Okay." He tried not to show his disappointment. "I'm sure it will come in time. Tell me more about what you do remember. Chet Walker offering you the gum and doing a lot of talking. Do you remember what he was talking about?"

"Not really. Most of it is a blur. The thing is, he was talking, and then he suddenly went quiet. I'm not sure if it was something I said or did, but he gave me this strange look and I got scared. I thought maybe he was going to hurt me."

"Did he threaten you?"

"No. I can't explain why I was scared. I just was. We were driving on this deserted mountain road, and I asked him to stop and let me out."

"And what did he do?"

"He said it wouldn't be safe. He just kept driving. And then I panicked. I think I started screaming. I grabbed the steering wheel. I only wanted him to pull over. But I guess I must have pulled too hard." Joelle covered her face with her hands. "I caused the accident. It's my fault that truck driver died."

Joelle started shaking. Clearly she was too distraught to eat or drink anything, so Wade put some cash on the table, then drove her to the twenty-four-hour medical clinic.

Thanks to the early hour the clinic wasn't busy and Joelle was in to see a doctor within fifteen minutes. As he waited, Wade thought about Chet Walker. If the man had been trying to do a good deed by giving a woman in distress a lift, he'd been poorly recompensed for his efforts.

Not that Wade could be sure Chet's intentions had been honorable. Joelle's memories at this point were still pretty patchy. And he couldn't be sure that what she did remember was accurate. Still, the scenario she'd described did fit with the facts and provide an explanation for the accident that at least made sense.

Twenty minutes later Dr. Blake—whom Wade had met more than a few times in the course of his duties—escorted Joelle to the reception room.

"Morning Sheriff. Joelle, here, is suffering emotional distress. She told me about the accident, the amnesia and the returning memories. Anyone would be upset going through something like this. The good news is that physically she appears fine. I've given her a prescription to control her anxiety. I suggest she take things easy for the rest of the day. Moderate exercise, like a walk on the beach, plus a few healthy meals, and she should be much better."

Once outside, seated in his SUV, Wade asked Joelle if she'd like him to drive her to Ashland. "Your husband is anxious to see you. Maybe once you're home again, all your memories will come back."

"I'm not sure I want that," Joelle said quietly.

"At one time we thought your husband might have beaten you. Because of the bruises." Wade glanced at the very faint mark on her upper arm that was almost gone now.

"Yes."

"But I spoke to Richard yesterday and he said you got those bruises at a self-defense class. Do you remember that?"

"No."

He let out a long breath. "We checked and you were registered for the class. You went to two sessions last week." He'd hoped that one memory would trigger the others. But it didn't seem to be working that way.

Wade thought of the photos in his pocket. If he showed them to her he might provoke another anxiety attack. But that baby had to be found.

He drove back to Frosty's, picked up their pastries and drinks in to-go cups, then suggested they sit on the beach to eat.

It was not yet nine and while people were stirring in town, the beach was still quiet. Just one family—a couple with two small children—had staked a spot on the beach. The father was putting up an umbrella, while the mother ran after the kids with a tube of sunscreen.

Wade avoided them, found a log farther down the beach where they could enjoy the warmth of the sun on their backs and the cool breeze off the ocean on their faces. He waited until Joelle had finished her tea and her muffin, then he pulled out the photos.

"I'm hoping these will help you remember. This is a picture of you and your husband. We found it at your cottage on Hyatt Lake. It was on the fridge."

She looked at him blankly, as if none of those words— husband, cottage, Hyatt Lake—meant anything to her.

He pressed the photo on her. She touched it with her fingertips, then withdrew as if she'd been shocked.

"I don't want to see that."

"You don't want to remember?"

"I'm scared."

"We need to find your baby, Joelle." He took out the second photo and a gust of wind almost pulled it out of his hand.

He used his second hand to shield it from the elements and placed it practically under her nose. A quick glance was all she gave it.

"I don't remember." She folded over at the waist, her face covered by her hands. "I'm sorry. I just can't."

* * *

"Hard to believe only one week ago I had time to go fishing." Wade was at the Linger Longer having a beer and sharing a pizza with Dougal and Charlotte. They'd invited him to their table when he'd walked in ten minutes ago, after a long, hard day.

But he supposed the day must have seemed longer, and harder for Joelle.

After their talk on the beach, he'd called Dunne into the office to take her statement about the accident. And then Detective Waverman had driven in from Ashland, and spent over an hour interrogating her, as well.

Hadn't done any good though.

She didn't remember anything about her life in Ashland, or, more importantly, her baby.

At least, that was what she told them. For the first time Wade had doubts. Doubts that were shared by Waverman who'd said, "She's faking, trying to make us feel sorry for her. I'll bet that poor kid is dead, probably buried on the property somewhere. Or at the bottom of the lake."

They'd both glanced at the photo of Josephine. Wade had tacked it up on the board in his office. Josephine looked plump, healthy and happy. Like a kid who'd been well taken care of.

She had a round face with a dimple in her button of a chin. Four tiny baby teeth peeked out from her smile. She had Joelle's blue eyes.

"Maybe you should switch careers," Dougal said. "Become a full time writer, like me. I've had plenty of free time this week."

"Hard enough keeping up with my own paperwork. Write an entire book? No thanks." Wade took another slice of the loaded pizza.

"So how's the new book coming?" Dougal might be preaching the joys of the writing life, but at the moment he looked rather discontented.

"Frankly, it's not."

Charlotte put a commiserating hand on Dougal's back. "He's got a great idea for a new mystery series. Fictional this time."

"But—turns out I suck at fiction."

"It's only been a week." Charlotte picked an olive off her pizza and set it aside.

"Plus I had a call from my agent today. I'd sent her an outline of the new project. She wasn't sure my publisher or fans are ready for the new direction. Might have been a tactful way of telling me the new story sucks."

"Maybe you should go back to the story about the librarians." Wade thought it was a reasonable suggestion, not worthy of the raised eyebrow of warning he got from Charlotte.

"One librarian is enough for me right now." Dougal fingered a strand of Charlotte's hair, and the two of them exchanged one of the looks the bar was famous for—lingering.

Charlotte was the first to break eye contact. Her cheeks were pink when she asked Wade how things were going with Joelle. "I take it they still haven't found her baby?"

"You've heard about that?" The news hadn't taken long to percolate through town.

"Of course I have. Joelle is all anyone has been talking about since the accident." Charlotte paused for a sip of her beer. "I can't understand why she's still here. Why doesn't she go home to Ashland and her husband?"

"Joelle still doesn't remember her husband, the child—or her life there at all. She doesn't want to go and we can't force her."

Charlotte eyed Dougal thoughtfully. "I wonder how she ended up here, of all places. Hometown of Dougal Lachlan, her favorite author."

Wade leaned in closer to block out the voices at the next table. "She tell you Dougal was her favorite author?"

"She came in today, wanting to see him. Apparently someone at the salon told her he sometimes worked at the library. And earlier in the week, she came to the library to borrow one of his books."

"*A Murder in the Family*—is that the one she wanted?" Wade could picture it on her nightstand at the shelter, and at the cottage too.

"Yes. How did you know?"

"Let's just say in the course of my investigation that book has come up a few times. It's a case about a man who kills his wife, isn't it?" He directed the question at Dougal, who didn't seem all that flattered by the attention.

"It is. The guy was so upstanding in the community he'd practically been given a halo. No one believed he was guilty but me and the wife's mother, at first."

"That's right." Wade was remembering now. Dougal's book had actually revamped public interest in the case, and turned up interesting evidence that had helped lead to the man's conviction.

"Maybe Joelle thought you could help her nail her husband this time," Charlotte speculated.

"But for what?" Dougal asked. "She isn't dead."

"But maybe the baby is." Charlotte shivered. "I'm sorry I said that. I'm afraid speculation is getting out of hand about this. And I'm becoming one of the worst gossips."

"I had no idea life was so eventful here in Twisted Cedars," Dougal said.

"It wasn't until you moved back," Wade pointed out.

"Well, at least Joelle has taken some of the heat off the Quinpools," Charlotte said. "I'm thinking of bringing Cory and Chester home again in a few days." Charlotte glanced at Dougal, as if trying to gauge his reaction.

Dougal looked unperturbed. "They've got to face their friends and neighbors sometime. Can't keep hiding in camp waiting for people to forget. Cause that sure as hell won't happen."

Charlotte turned to Wade. "Any chance you could tell us what's going on with that case? Do you think Kyle is going to be arrested? I'd hate for them to be here for that."

Wade shook his head. "You know I can't say. But if I was you, I'd let them stay in that camp for one more week."

* * *

Wade was leaving the Linger Longer when a call came in from Terri Morrison at Heartland.

"Sheriff. Glad I caught you."

"How can I help?" He could tell by her rapid fire speech something was wrong.

"We've just sent Joelle Caruthers by ambulance to Brookings. She's been acting erratically since she came back from the Sheriff's Office. And then she just sort of crumbled onto the floor and started crying. Wouldn't let anyone touch her."

Wade cursed. He'd sensed she was at the breaking point that morning. Dealing with Detective Waverman must have pushed her over the edge.

"Thanks for letting me know, Terri." He disconnected the call, then got into his SUV. For a while he pondered where he should go. It was eight o'clock. Home wasn't out of the question.

But he drove right by the turnoff that would take him there, and ended up on the highway heading south to Brookings. What the hell. He wouldn't sleep anyway.

chapter twenty-eight

At the Brookings Hospital, Wade had to wait for two hours to talk to Dr. Schrock. He wasn't allowed to visit Joelle, which was just as well.

He had to protect whatever objectivity he still possessed. So many people—including his colleagues—suspected her of faking her memory loss. They thought she knew what had happened to her baby—that possibly she was the one who had harmed her.

Initially Wade had been sure it was the husband.

There was the wedding ring—possibly flung on the floor during an argument. The fact that Richard hadn't made time to call his family at all during the week they were at the cottage.

But learning about Joelle's self-defense class had shifted his perspective. He'd checked in with the instructor and learned that the last two sessions had been pretty physical—which could account for Joelle's bruising.

The question was—whom had she felt she needed to defend herself from? Her husband...or someone else?

Wade was grabbing a coffee from the vending machine when Dr. Schrock strode into the waiting room. Her long blond hair was secured in a ponytail, and behind her dark-framed glasses, her eyes looked tired.

"Joelle is sleeping now. It may be some time before she's strong enough to talk to you or anyone else."

He could hear the admonishment behind the words. Dr. Schrock blamed them for getting Joelle into this state. "You're aware we're trying to find her baby?"

Dr. Schrock's eyes widened. "When the paramedics brought her in, we were told she'd been identified as Joelle

Caruthers from Ashland, but that her memory still hadn't returned. No one mentioned a baby."

"Her name is Josephine and she's ten-months old. Joelle and Josephine spent last week at their family cottage on Lake Hyatt. When her husband arrived this past Friday morning, he found them both missing."

"Dear god." Dr. Schrock pushed back on the bridge of her glasses. "This changes everything."

Wade agreed. "Joelle called me early this morning to tell me she remembered what had caused the accident. She'd asked the driver to pull over and when he wouldn't, she'd grabbed the wheel, not intending any harm, but just to force him to listen to her."

The neurologist looked thoughtful. "What else did she remember?"

"Not much. She couldn't tell me how she'd ended up in the truck with him. And she still had no memory of her life before that moment. Is this sort of partial memory returning normal?"

"Generally the memory returns in bits and pieces, yes. But in every case I've seen, generally the accident that caused the impairment is the last to return. In many cases the victim never remembers it at all."

"Could she be faking her amnesia?"

"She wasn't very lucid when she came in tonight. But based on my examination last week, I'd say she presented with behavior and symptoms very typical of amnesia brought on by a trauma."

Wade took a sip of the coffee. It was awful. He took another sip anyway. How could he make sense of the fact that Joelle had remembered the accident that had caused her amnesia—and yet couldn't recall anything else?

"Unless we were right, earlier, when we speculated the trauma that caused Joelle's memory loss wasn't the truck accident—but something that happened earlier that day."

* * *

day 9 after the accident

Wade managed to catch four hours of sleep Saturday night, but he was awakened early the next morning by a call from Detective Waverman.

"Mackay here." He put on the speakerphone so he could pull on his sweatpants.

"Sorry to call so early. But I wanted to give you the latest update. We finally managed to track down the neighbors who live closest to the Caruthers on the lake." Waverman sounded tense. Exhausted.

Undoubtedly his team would be working around the clock as long as there was a chance the baby could be alive. "Did they see anything?"

"The husband said he heard a boat motor fire up around midnight, a week ago last Friday. This was pretty unusual, so he got out of bed and looked out the window. He claimed he saw Richard and Joelle drive off in their runabout. He's pretty sure Joelle had the baby in her arms, but all he had to see by was moonlight, so he can't be sure."

"How far from his window to the Caruthers's dock?"

"About two hundred yards."

"So he can't be sure the people were Richard, Joelle and the baby."

"But he's sure about the boat."

"Did he hear them return?"

"No. He claims he went back to bed and didn't wake up again until morning. By then the boat was back where it belonged. He said everything was quiet when he and his wife left to go to Medford for a week. Their daughter just had a baby."

Wade went to the kitchen and set the phone on the counter while he put on a pot of coffee. "So midnight on the Friday in question, two people, one possibly holding a baby, took the Caruthers's boat out on the lake. Have you had a chance to question Richard?"

"He's sticking to his story that he was home in Ashland by nine o'clock. He says he kept the key to the boat in a drawer at the cottage. And it's still there. We've sent it in to check for fingerprints."

"So if he's telling the truth—who was the man in the boat?"

"We've been interviewing neighbors, and tracing Joelle's phone calls. So far nothing. If she was having an affair, she never called the guy. There are no registered offenders in the vicinity. No leads on who this guy could be, other than the obvious."

Richard Caruthers.

"By the way, Joelle suffered a breakdown at the women's shelter last night. She's been admitted into Brookings Medical Center."

Waverman cursed. "We need her getting better, not worse."

* * *

Wade showered, got dressed, then took a cup of coffee out to the deck. His mom had been quite the gardener. Every year since she'd left, the yard looked a little sadder. He kept the hedge pruned, lawns mowed, and perennial beds weeded, but he lacked the finer skills of staking and dividing. Which meant the delphiniums were bowed like supplicants and the daisies were taking over almost everything else.

Maybe he should be like Dougal. Buy a place in the woods and not bother with all this.

But Wade liked living in town. He enjoyed his neighbors and being able to walk to the Linger Longer from his home if he wished. And normally he found it relaxing to putter around the yard. This summer, though, he hadn't had much time.

Summer was always a challenging time for law enforcement, thanks to the influx of tourists and outdoor recreationalists. But this summer had been extra brutal.

Ever since Dougal arrived.

Dougal was the one who'd found Daisy Hammond-Quinpool's remains.

And Dougal had gotten everyone worked up about the librarian murders that occurred in the seventies and a possible connection to Charlotte's aunt Shirley.

The truck accident and Joelle's amnesia and missing child was the one serious case that didn't seem to have any connection to Dougal.

And yet, his book was on Joelle's nightstand—both at the cottage and in the women's shelter. And according to Charlotte, Joelle seemed fixated on a need to see Dougal again.

Wade rested his head against the chair and closed his eyes. As he relaxed, he recalled simpler times. The high school years. Back then he and Dougal had been on the same football team, along with Kyle Quinpool who'd played quarterback. Wade had been the middle line-backer. Dougal the safety. They'd played well together, in fact it had seemed at times like they could read each other's minds.

Off the field, their relationship had been more complicated.

Wade had always thought Kyle lay at the root of the problem. Confident and entitled, Kyle had been into wild parties, reckless driving and casual hookups behind Daisy's back. Wade had tried to restrain him, but Dougal had seemed to feed on Kyle's insanity—at least he had when he was a teenager.

They'd had many a fight over trouble that Kyle started.

But maybe the root of their differences had been deeper.

Recently Dougal had told him that he'd always felt an outsider. He lived in a trailer park on the west side of town. His mom cleaned house for Wade and Kyle's families. Worse, he had a father who was estranged from the family and was serving time for murder.

That had been the real cause of their differences, Wade suspected.

But could any of that history have relevance to what was going on in Twisted Cedars right now?

Wade didn't see how. Yet, he felt that it might.

* * *

At three in the afternoon Wade was at his office catching up on paperwork, when he got another call from a grim-voiced Detective Waverman.

"We've recovered the body of a baby same approximate age, sex and size as Josephine Caruthers."

The words hit Wade like a punch in the gut. Kids, especially babies, were always the hardest. "Have you got a positive ID?"

"Medical Examiner can't say for sure. But the father has identified the pajamas she was wearing at the time."

"Winnie-the Pooh," Wade recalled.

"That's right."

"Cause of death is drowning?"

There was a pause, then Waverman shared a fact that wouldn't be going public. "That's for your ears only. We'll have the preliminary autopsy tomorrow. For now all we're saying is the body had been in the water for about a week."

"You've got someone notifying the mother?" He thought of Joelle, vulnerable and damaged in her hospital room. How would this news affect her? Would she be protected from pain by her broken-down brain?

Was whatever had happened to Josephine the reason she'd broken down in the first place?

"Any leads on the guy who was driving the boat?"

"We've talked to the neighbor again. He says for sure it was a man. But he admits he can't say for sure it was Richard."

"How did the husband react when you told him his daughter's body had been recovered?"

This was a key moment for a trained investigator. If the husband had been guilty, there were numerous ways he might betray himself.

"He broke down and cried."

Like a normal father.

Like an innocent man.

Then again, Richard Caruthers was in the theatre business. They couldn't afford to forget that.

chapter twenty-nine

day 10 after the accident

monday morning Jamie asked Colin Howard if she could talk to him about her future with the firm.

She'd spent most of the weekend thinking about the house on Horizon Hill Road.

Twice she'd driven by it. The third time, she'd gone out and walked the length of the road, studying the houses of the neighbors and trying to decide if she would fit in.

She knew her brother thought she—and their mother— were eternal optimists with a weakness for being too trusting, a soft touch. He blamed their soft hearts for their bad judgment in men. And he'd been proved right on that score.

But what he didn't seem to appreciate was that she and her mother also shared a realistic streak.

Dougal judged their mother harshly for her casual affairs. Never had it occurred to him that their mother had been protecting them, not letting any man close enough to ever hurt her children.

Their mother had made her own happily ever after her own bad marriage.

Now Jamie had to do the same thing.

"Let's talk now." Colin got up to close the door. At fifty-two, Colin was the 'younger' of the firm's two partners. In the past he'd hinted broadly that he could foresee the day when Jamie would be invited to be a full-equity partner, too. She had no idea if the drama in her life over the two months had affected her chances.

She hoped not.

"I'm really grateful you and Ben let me come back to the firm when my marriage ended. But I need to know what you're prepared to offer for the future."

"You're a great asset to the firm." Ben looked at her with warm brown eyes—they always seemed to be smiling, even when his mouth wasn't. "Eventually we'd like to see you in a partner role. Down the road."

"I'm just wondering how far down the road. And if we could get something in writing."

Colin's eyebrows went up.

Jamie worried she'd come across as too pushy. "Since I've already sold my trailer, I don't have anywhere to live. I could buy another trailer with my money. But I looked at a house on Horizon Hill Road this weekend. It's lovely, but I wouldn't want to buy unless I was sure I had a secure future here."

Colin nodded approvingly. "A house in that neighborhood would be a good investment for you. Even more importantly, I think it's a healthy step."

He hesitated, then sighed. "What Kyle did—we were all shocked Jamie. No one guessed he was capable of something like that. I feel terrible that he managed to deceive you as well."

Jamie noticed he spoke definitely, as if there were no doubt. Innocent until proven guilty was merely a technicality in this case, and in this town.

Not that she blamed Colin, or anyone else. Kyle had pretty much admitted his guilt, straight to her face. And the facts were difficult to dispute.

"I don't want to be pitied, Colin. I just want to ensure I'm making a sound financial commitment if I make an offer on this house."

"Fair enough. You've earned nothing but respect in this office. In fact, we were just talking about assigning you a new client. We've been approached by a wealthy individual looking for a new tax accountant. Ben and I both agreed you would be perfect."

This was better than she'd hoped. "Really?"

"Yes. It's time you started building your own client base. I think it's fair to say that in five years you would be in position to be named Junior Partner. How does that sound?"

"Excellent. Thanks Colin." She would call Bailey Landax on her lunch hour. Talk about putting together an offer. Jamie could feel her spirits lifting.

But then Colin shared another piece of news.

"Did you hear Kyle and Jim have put their real estate business on the market? Can't say I'm surprised. I heard all their clients are asking to be let out of their agreements. Needless to say, they haven't closed a deal since the news went public."

"I hadn't heard."

"I guess they aren't expecting the trouble to blow over."

"No. I don't think there's much chance of that happening."

* * *

Headlines kept distracting Charlotte as she put out the Monday morning editions in the Newspaper and Periodical section of the library.

"Baby's Body Found in Hyatt Lake."

"Hopes Die As Baby's Body Discovered."

The local Oregon papers had been covering the story of the Caruthers' missing child all weekend, but on Monday the news went national. Even the *New York Times* and *Washington Post* made mention of it, though not on the front page.

Charlotte read every story, even though they all said essentially the same thing.

And they all played up the bit about the Winnie the Pooh pajamas. The fact that the tiny corpse had been wearing them seemed to leave little room for doubt that the recovered body truly was little Josephine Caruthers.

Charlotte returned to her desk where she added two new titles to her wish list. There were so many great books she wanted to buy for the library this fall—if only she had a bigger acquisitions budget. But as the board kept reminding her, more people came to the library to use the free Wi-Fi than they did to read books now. It was a changing world, and libraries had to change, as well.

"Look at this one!" A skinny girl with light brown hair giggled as she hit the play button on a You Tube video. Her friend, sitting on a chair that had been squished into the same cubicle, leaned forward. "Oh, they're so cute!"

Casually Charlotte checked the screen as she walked past, and smiled as she saw that the girls were watching a video about cats. The two girls, around age thirteen, had been online for about an hour now. Though the computers were highly protected, Charlotte still liked to keep an eye on them.

At three o'clock all the online news services were beeping with updates on the Caruthers' case. Preliminary autopsy results confirmed the little girl's identity and pointed to drowning as the cause of death, probably late Friday night or early Saturday morning.

Charlotte called Dougal. "Did you hear the latest on Joelle's baby?"

"I just got in from a hike on some old logging roads."

Which meant the writing wasn't going well. Again.

Charlotte had initially supported the idea of him writing a fictional mystery. But she was beginning to think Dougal had another calling. One he might hate, but that he couldn't deny.

"You still there? You said there was news about the baby?"

She relayed the autopsy results. "The reporters are also quoting a neighbor who saw Joelle and her husband take the baby out on the boat around midnight a week ago Friday. Do you think they killed her together?"

"And then Richard goes back to Ashland and resumes working like usual—while Joelle walks down to the highway and hitches a ride with a trucker? Doesn't make sense."

"No. It really doesn't." She hung up the phone, worried about Joelle, sad for the baby...and worried about Dougal, as well.

* * *

Monday, from start to finish, was crazy at the Curry County Sheriff's Office.

The trouble started when Laura and Vern Anders of Port Orford were reported missing. Both of their employers phoned the Sheriff's Office, independently, out of concern when they didn't show up for work as usual.

Apparently they were model employees who never took sick days. Certainly not without phoning in to apologize.

One of Laura's co-workers recounted Laura saying she and her husband planned to camp at Illahe and hike the Upper Rogue River Trail on the weekend.

Wade assigned the search and rescue mission to Dunne. "Might as well set up a command post at the Campground. Round up as many officers and volunteers as you can."

"Will do." Dunne marched out of his office with as much speed as he was capable of.

An hour later he reported that they'd found the Ander's vehicle and tent at the campground. No sign of Laura or Vern, however.

"God, I hope we find them alive and well," Wade muttered, when Marnie came in with some requests for him to sign.

"Laura Ander's co-worker told me Laura was nervous because she'd heard there were lots of black bears, cougars and rattlesnakes on the trail." Marnie rolled her eyes.

Only amateur hikers would worry about the wildlife indigenous to the Coastal Mountain terrain. Seasoned pros didn't blink twice over the existence of wildlife. The animals were out there. If you were smart, and took a few precautions, they caused no problems.

Within three hours Dunne called in another progress report. They had searchers in place, working their way up the Rogue River Trail. He'd also been tracking down other hikers and river rafters who'd been on the trail Sunday. So far none of them had recognized photos of the Anders.

"Seems like they must have gone off the trail fairly early in the day," Dunne concluded.

When Marnie set a sandwich and coffee on his desk, Wade glanced at his watch. Already it was two. "Thanks."

"There's too much going on these days to have our sheriff collapsing from weakness. I hear there's a new restaurant opening at the look out on the point. Menu sounds great. And the views would be amazing."

"Thanks for the tip. Come September I may have time to check it out." He looked over Marnie's shoulder. Duane was in the doorway, waving a sheaf of papers.

"Lab results."

Wade waved him inside, and Marnie withdrew.

"Human hair found on the tarp that had been wrapped around Daisy Hammond's body prior to burial, and on Daisy, herself, has been DNA matched to Kyle Quinpool," Duane reported. He flipped to another page.

"And the blood in the Quinpool's kitchen is a match to Daisy's, as well."

Wade let it all soak in. While the results were as expected, it was still sobering to reflect that their case was now as solid as it would ever get.

Jim's confession the other day had been a smokescreen. The fact that he hadn't even known what Daisy was wearing had confirmed to Wade that Kyle had acted alone. When you took these lab results, added the fraud Kyle had perpetrated with Daisy's bank card, and the known tension between him and his ex-wife, the case looked pretty strong.

They'd just have to see if the prosecutor agreed.

chapter thirty

dougal was bothered more than he thought he should be by news of Joelle Caruthers' baby's death. He'd planned to try writing again that afternoon, but his thoughts kept veering away from his fiction and circling back to Joelle.

Was it really a coincidence that she'd ended up in his hometown?

It wasn't logical to think there might be a connection between them. He knew he'd never met her before. But he couldn't stop thinking that she must have thought he could help her. And for that to be true, there had to be a reason.

Had it been something he'd written in his book?

Or was it something more personal. Something he'd overlooked.

The more he ruminated, the more he feared he'd let her down. She was an emotionally battered woman, in need of help. A woman running from her identity in more ways than one.

And then an idea came to him.

He went online to read about the homicide case that had landed his father in prison ten-and-a-half years ago. He searched until he saw photos of the victim.

And when he did, he realized he might be onto something.

He called Wade. "Look, I have a hunch about Joelle Caruthers. Would it be possible for you to tell me everything you know about her background?"

"That's not the way the system works." Wade sounded bone-tired. "We do the interviewing. Not the general public."

"Sometimes you have to be flexible."

"I'm juggling a dozen problems at the moment. Is that flexible enough for you?"

"If I'm right, Joelle's life could be in danger. You want to follow the system? Or save her?"

Of course Wade could only make one choice.

"Linger Longer in an hour?"

"I'll be there," Dougal promised.

* * *

Wade looked like a burdened man when he entered the bar at the agreed upon time. Dougal had a light beer and a burger waiting for him. Personally, he had no appetite, and his own beer was on the table, untouched. He wanted to keep a clear head.

"Thanks for coming."

Wade sank heavily into his chair. "We may be too late already."

"What happened?"

"I just had a call from the clinic in Brookings. Joelle left without checking out.

"Do you have any idea where she's headed? Or if she's alone?"

Wade shook his head.

"Did she know the baby's body had been found?"

"Yes. Someone on staff at the hospital told her. And she disappeared about an hour later. Maybe the shock of having the death confirmed brought back more of her memories and she just couldn't deal. I wish like hell she would have called me, if she needed help."

"Is it possible she didn't leave the hospital of her own accord?"

"I wondered about that. I called the authorities in Ashland to see if they could question Richard. But they can't find him. I'm afraid he may be the one who took Joelle out of that hospital."

Dougal had another theory. But he needed more information, first.

When he noticed Wade examining the beer and burger in front of him like they were puzzling artifacts, he said, "Eat. You're going to need your strength."

Without apparent enthusiasm Wade took a bite of the burger and washed it down with a drink of water, not beer.

"So what can you tell me about Joelle?"

"You really think this will help?"

"I do."

Wade sighed. "What the hell. Situation can't get much worse. Joelle's mother died when she was a young girl, and she ended up in foster care."

"Her father?" Dougal asked quietly.

"Wasn't in the picture. That's according to Richard."

Dougal could hear the blood pounding in his ears. "Tell me about the baby. How did she die?"

Wade shifted in his chair. "The body was found in the lake. We won't have the autopsy report until tomorrow."

Dougal stared at him. The eyes of an honest man always revealed more than the man himself. "You know more than that."

Wade hesitated for a long time before admitting, "There is something we're keeping from the public."

"The baby had a broken neck, right?"

Wade stiffened with shock. And it was his turn to search Dougal's eyes for the truth.

"I'll tell you my theory," Dougal said. "But you're going to think I'm crazy."

"Try me."

"I think Joelle is my half-sister. I'm afraid our father killed her baby. And he may be going after Joelle as well."

* * *

Dougal was waiting to see how Wade would reply to his theory, when he realized Wade was no longer focusing on their conversation, but was eyeing a stranger who'd just entered the bar.

The man was average looking in every sense except for a prominent chin. His clothing set him apart from most locals—linen pants and a light pink shirt.

Dougal had a hunch. "Is that Richard Caruthers?"

"Yup." Wade had locked eyes with the other man, and waited as Richard strode over purposefully.

Richard splayed his hands on the table, showing off a polished wedding ring and a fairly recent manicure.

"Where is my wife? I need to see her."

"Sit down," Wade invited. "Let's talk."

"The person I need to talk to is my wife. I was just at the hospital, but they told me she wasn't there. That she hadn't been checked out, she'd just left."

"I heard the same thing. But I don't know where she is. We've put out an APB—hopefully she'll be found soon."

Richard's lips trembled. He took the proffered chair. "I don't know what to do."

"You've had a hard day. I'm sorry about your daughter."

Richard shielded his eyes with his hand, accepting the condolences with a slight nod.

After a while Wade made introductions. "Richard, this is a friend of mine, Dougal Lachlan. He already knows who you are."

"I know him, too." Richard lowered his hand and gazed at Dougal. "You're my wife's favorite author. She has all your books at home. She's always talking about going to meet you one day."

"We actually did meet a few days ago. But given her confused mental state, I'm not sure she'll remember."

"It's so hard for me to believe she doesn't remember me. Or Josephine. How could such a thing be possible—?"

"I was talking to the neurologist yesterday," Wade said. "We began to wonder if the event that caused Joelle's confusion and memory loss might have been something that happened before the truck accident. In which case her head injury exacerbated an already existing medical condition."

"And this traumatic incident—you think it's Josephine's death?"

Wade nodded.

"I know I told that other detective that she'd been worried and distracted the past few weeks. But I don't believe she had anything to do with our daughter's death. She doted on Josephine. We both did."

"I don't think Joelle hurt Josephine," Dougal said. "I believe it was the man who took them out on the boat on Friday night who did it."

"It wasn't me!" Richard's denial was heated and instant. Dougal guessed he'd been questioned repeatedly, until the whole subject was raw.

"I never meant to imply it was you," Dougal said. "Have you ever met Joelle's father?"

Richard frowned. "No. They were estranged. She refused to talk about him."

"Did she ever tell you how her mother died?"

"Car crash. Why are you asking about Joelle's parents?"

Wade glanced uncertainly at Dougal. Dougal could tell he was questioning the theory about Joelle being the daughter of Ed Lachlan and his second wife. When Wade narrowed his eyes at him, Dougal could tell he was warning him not to say anything to Richard.

So he didn't. But as he was leaving, he said quietly, so only Wade could hear. "Ask the cops in Ashland to check Joelle's email. See if she ever got messages from Librarianmomma."

Wade sucked in a breath. "Christ. You think she did?"

"I do. And I'll bet they started a couple of weeks ago. About the time she registered for that self-defense course."

* * *

After his meeting with Dougal, Wade went out to the Illahe Campground to check in on the search for Laura and Vern Anders. He arrived just as the news was going out that the couple had been found, ten miles up the river and a mile off the trail.

They'd become disoriented three hours into their hike on Sunday, and then Laura twisted her ankle. She made the mistake of taking off her boot and then couldn't get it back on. They'd spent the night seven miles from their campground and had been hobbling around in circles for most of the next day.

Wade thanked his staff and volunteers for their work, then congratulated Dunne on a job well done.

"Talk about clueless," Dunne complained. "They were one mile from the river for God's sake. All they had to do was find the river and follow it downstream to the campground."

"Hopefully they'll take a compass with them on their next trip." Wade was just glad they'd found people, and not bodies. The paperwork would be a lot lighter.

Back in his SUV, Wade checked his messages. Reports had come in from two separate witnesses who had seen a woman who resembled Joelle leaving the hospital that morning with an older man.

The older man was described as wearing a wide brimmed Tilley hat, and sandy colored hiking pants and shirt. In other words, he looked like half the older tourists in Oregon right now.

Wade's staff was tired and stretched thin after the search for the hikers. But he needed bodies out on the street, looking for Joelle.

If Dougal's crazy theory was right, the older man with Joelle could be Ed Lachlan.

And if Ed had killed Josephine, it stood to reason Joelle was now in danger, too.

chapter thirty-one

day 11 after the accident

On Tuesday morning, Jamie made Stella coffee and toast. She wasn't going into the office today. She had an appointment with her realtor in the morning, and then she was driving down to meet her new client.

"Where's Amos?" Though she'd been living in their house for several weeks now, it seemed she rarely saw him.

"He was up early. Don't know where he took off."

When had Amos started avoiding his own house, his own wife? Jamie didn't know the answer to that question and she was nervous to broach the subject with Stella. Maybe it was easier for her to just pretend everything was normal between her and her husband. Even though it obviously wasn't.

As she waited for her toast to pop, Jamie glanced out at the backyard. "That old tree house still looks in good shape."

"It is. The neighbor kids play up there sometimes. When Amos builds something, he builds it to last."

Jamie glanced at the older woman, wondering if there was a hidden meaning in her last sentence. But Stella was unconcernedly putting jam on her toast.

"I've heard rumors Kyle is going to be arrested soon. Maybe even today."

"I've heard the same thing," Jamie admitted.

"Have you decided to go ahead with the annulment?"

Jamie didn't answer.

"You feel bad for him don't you?"

"Yeah. I sort of do. Even though I know I shouldn't."

"That's fine. That's who you are. But you need to make your decision based on what will make *you* happy."

Jamie slathered peanut butter on her toast, added cream to her coffee. "What makes you think I won't?"

"I knew your mother, and you're just like her. When Edward was having his tempers and getting rough with her, all Katie could think about was how to make him happy. *What am I doing wrong?* She would ask me, and she never believed me when I said *nothing*. The only reason she kicked him out was to protect you kids. She never would have done it for herself."

Jamie had heard this story many times already. "But Kyle has never hurt me, Stella. And he doesn't have a terrible temper, either."

But he did have a way of going all cold and silent when he was disappointed and that was almost worse than being yelled at. No sense telling Stella that, though. She didn't need any more ammunition in her war against Jamie's marriage.

"There's lots of kinds of hurting, Jamie."

"I'm sure you're right. And I bet most marriages have at least a little of that to contend with." She almost added *even you and Amos*. But she didn't need to. She could see the flash of pain in Stella's eyes that was quickly replaced with concern.

"Don't think I take marriage vows lightly. I don't. But you have to consider what you have invested. You and Kyle have only been together a short while in the scheme of things. You haven't bought a house together, or made any other big investments. And you don't have children. No one could blame you for wanting a clean start. You're not even thirty. You could still have the life you've dreamed of—a good husband, a happy home and children of your own."

She may not have realized it, but Stella had hit on the sorest point from Jamie's point of view. Kyle had made it clear when he asked her to marry him that he didn't want more children. Two were enough and he hoped that she could grow to love them as if they were her own.

Loving Chester and Cory hadn't been a problem. Accepting that she would have no babies of her own was.

But she'd agreed to those terms when she'd married him.

And on one point Stella was wrong. Chester and Cory might not be Jamie's biological children. But she knew they loved her as much as she loved them. The decision she made about whether to remain a part of their family would have lasting repercussions on their lives.

"I see that expression on your face. You're thinking I don't know what I'm talking about."

Jamie flushed.

"Well I do. When Amos and I got married, I had as much hope for our future as you did when you married Kyle."

"Stella—"

"Don't try and stop me. And don't look at your watch and tell me you need to get to the office. By the time you're finished eating that toast, I'll be done. It doesn't take much to derail a marriage. Sometimes the small pebble in your shoe at the start of a journey is the one that ends up making the most painful blister."

"Kyle's lies weren't exactly small pebbles."

"My point exactly." Stella patted her hand. "I always said you were a smart one."

* * *

The glass door to the library was smashed in when Charlotte arrived for work on Tuesday morning.

She gasped. Then dropped her keys and spent almost an entire minute staring at the door, as if the image before her would reform itself.

But the glass remained broken.

She called Dougal first. He and Borden had spent the night at her place. When she'd left him this morning, he'd said he was going for a walk on the beach.

She suspected he was still looking for Joelle. He'd been all over town the previous evening trying to find her.

"Dougal. I'm so glad you answered. There's been a break-in at the library."

He swore. "Where are you?"

"At the front door. I was just about to unlock it when I saw the broken glass."

"Don't go inside. Come home Charlotte. I'll call 911."

"But I'll need to be here when the police arrive. So I can tell them what's missing. And assess the damage. Oh, and call the insurance company. And—" Her head swam at the prospect of all that would need to be done.

"Listen. Come home. Now."

She frowned.

"I'm on the beach headed to Oceans Way. I'll be on Driftwood Lane in less than a minute. I expect to see you shortly. Now get off the line so I can call 911."

When she tried to press the end button, her finger was shaking so much she could hardly manage.

Shock, she supposed.

With a glance over her shoulder at the library—a building that wouldn't exist if not for the championing of her family—she started toward Ocean Way. Less than sixty seconds later she ran into Dougal.

He looked frantic.

"I'm fine," she assured him. "And the library building and contents are insured..."

But if he heard her, he wasn't reassured. He gave her a quick hug and a peck on the cheek.

"I'll call you soon," he said. "Just go home. Stay inside and lock the—"

He paused, then changed his mind. "On second thought, you better stay with me." He took her arm and they walked together, retracing her morning route to work.

By the time they arrived, Wade and Deputy Carter had their guns at ready. Wade motioned for them to stand back.

"Police! If anyone is in there, come out with hands high."

Charlotte shrank behind one of the twisted cedars. Dougal put a hand over her shoulders, and told her to prepare herself for something awful.

"What?"

Dougal's skin looked gray, his eyes welded to the front door.

The two law officers had disappeared inside. A few passersby stopped to ask what was wrong.

"We don't know yet," Dougal said. "But to be safe, I'd cross the road if I were you."

A few minutes later a second squad car arrived, this one with two more officers. One began cordoning off the area. The other went inside, calling out his name and asking if everything was okay.

When a third squad car arrived, followed by an ambulance, Charlotte didn't know what to think.

"What did they find in there?" She studied Dougal's face. "You know, don't you?"

"Everyone's been looking for Joelle since she left the hospital yesterday," he said. "I'm afraid she's in there."

"You think she broke into the library sometime last night?"

"No. I think Ed broke in."

Dougal had shared his theory with her last night. She'd listened without comment, not wanting to hurt his feelings and tell him how preposterous she found it.

The idea that Joelle was his half-sister and that Ed Lachlan would have tracked her down and killed her baby. Why, it was crazy. Besides, last time Dougal had seen him, his father had been in New York. Across the country. Why would he return to Oregon, where the likelihood of getting picked up for breaking his parole would be that much greater?

"I'm not following," she said. "Why would Ed want to go inside the library?"

"I'm afraid to answer that. All I know is that he is one sick bastard. I need to warn Jamie." He pulled out his phone, but ended up leaving a message. "Call me, Jamie. It's urgent."

When more than an hour had passed, Charlotte suggested they grab a coffee at Frosty's.

"You go ahead," Dougal said. "I can watch you from here."

"You think it's not safe for me to walk down Driftwood Lane in the middle of the morning?"

"Nothing's going to feel safe to me until I find out what happened in the library, and whether my father was involved.

chapter thirty-two

In 1976, Wade's father, who was then the Sheriff of Curry County, had been the first responder when the library's handyman, Amos Ward, reported finding the local librarian, Shirley Hammond, hanging from an exposed rafter in the basement, dead.

Now, twenty-four years later, it was Wade's turn.

Only, instead of Shirley Hammond, it was Joelle Caruthers who had died, hung from an exposed rafter, a stool knocked over at her feet.

Wade came close to breaking down when he first saw her.

And in that instant, he understood why his father had never gotten over Shirley Hammond's death.

He pulled himself together and, following protocol, told Duane call for back-up while he checked for vital signs—of which there were none. The body was cold and rigor was already setting in.

Later, he wasn't surprised when his deputy coroner estimated Joelle had been dead for at least eight hours.

While Wade's father had been given every reason to believe Shirley had committed suicide—there'd been an overturned stool by the body, as well as a library book open to instruction on how to hang yourself—Wade knew Joelle had been murdered.

"Two theories occur to me," Duane said, when the crime team was hard at work, and after the body had been removed. "One, her memory came back and she couldn't handle the fact that her baby was dead so she committed suicide."

Wade nodded. It was possible.

"Or, two, her husband wanted her dead and staged this to look like suicide."

"Richard Caruthers was in Twisted Cedars last night," Wade said. "I saw him at the Linger Longer. He flat out admitted he was looking for his wife." A stupid move for a man bent on murder.

"Obviously, he wasn't thinking straight. Probably half-crazed with grief and anger."

"That's a strong possibility. But Dougal Lachlan raised another option with me. He has a suspicion that Joelle might be the daughter from his father's second marriage. I sent some emails last night. Should find out today if it's true."

"Well that's weird. But is it relevant?"

"Apparently Ed Lachlan's claiming he murdered four librarians in the seventies. He may have been behind the apparent suicide of our local librarian back then as well."

"I've heard rumors about that," Carter admitted. "But say it's true. Why would he then murder his own daughter and grand-daughter?"

"That's a good question." It was diabolical, and perverted, that a woman and her child should die on the whim of a sick and twisted man.

But if it were true, it wouldn't be the first time.

No wonder Dougal was haunted by the fact that he shared DNA with this bastard. Suddenly Wade understood so much about Dougal that had eluded him before.

As soon as he was able, Wade went outside to see if Dougal and Charlotte were still waiting. He found them sitting on a bench by the twisted cedars, leaning in toward one another, heads touching. They were holding hands.

"Is it Joelle? Is she dead?" Charlotte asked.

"I'm afraid so."

Charlotte closed her eyes.

Dougal looked haunted. "It looks like suicide, I bet. But it isn't, my father did this, Wade."

"I'm checking into your theory that Joelle was Ed's daughter. But as you recall, Richard Caruthers was in town last night, too," Wade felt obliged to point out. "Looking for Joelle."

"The husband is always the first suspect, right?" Charlotte sounded like she wanted this to be true.

No doubt she hoped to spare Dougal the burden of assuming yet another sin of his father's.

"Usually," Wade said. "But even if Richard did want Joelle dead, it seems unlikely he would have tied together two red scarves to do the job."

chapter thirty-three

during her drive to Port Orford to sign an offer for the house on Horizon Hill Road, Jamie got a call from her brother. She let it go to messages. Kyle called next. She almost let it go as well, then decided she'd better answer.

"They're going to arrest me soon," Kyle said. "My lawyer thinks it will probably be today."

Jamie was silent. What could she say?

"Will you watch out for Cory and Chester?"

"Of course I will."

"Thanks. I realize I was out of the line the other day, asking if you would petition for custody. And I'll make things easy for you to apply for an annulment. I've had my lawyer draw up a statement where I admit to marrying you under fraudulent circumstances."

"Oh." Jamie was taken aback by his reasonableness. She was used to looking for the ulterior motive in everything Kyle said and did. "Thank you."

"I'm sorry for everything. I truly am. I realize from your perspective I've been a real shit. And you never deserved that."

His words freed her. Absolved her. She ought to be feeling relieved right now. So why were her eyes filling with tears.

"I just have one last favor to ask, Jamie."

Oh, oh. Here it comes. She took a deep breath, preparing herself for a blow of some sort.

"I know I lied and hid things from you, right from the start. But I did love you, Jamie. I still do. You don't owe me anything. But if you could try to believe that, I would really appreciate it."

"Good luck, Kyle," she managed to reply, before ending the call.

Tears filled her eyes and she blinked them away. It would be easier to deal with the end of this marriage if she could view Kyle as a villain, plain and simple.

But she just couldn't do that.

And this last conversation had reminded her of all the good things. Maybe she was a fool to believe him when he said he still loved her.

The truth was, she still felt love for him, too.

Along with anger, resentment and disappointment.

Still, she knew an annulment was the right step. And so was buying this house. She liked the idea of starting out in a new neighborhood, with a new place. She'd be in control of her life now. No more dreaming about a prince on a white steed, promising her a happily ever after.

Baily greeted Jamie at the door to her office dressed in a silk blouse and a summer-weight wool skirt. She'd had her gel nails redone. They were red now, with gold tips.

Jamie wondered if Bailey had intended the symbolism. Probably not.

"Would you like a coffee? Our receptionist can make you a latte or an espresso."

"A latte would be nice." She could use the caffeine. It had been a long day, and she still had another appointment after this one.

They sat down together in a small conference room with framed photographs of beautiful houses on the walls. Bailey was patient and thorough as she went through each clause of the agreement. Jamie had a nice down payment and an approved mortgage. The only condition to her offer was a home inspection—which shouldn't cause a problem in Bailey's opinion.

"The price we're offering is a little low, but it shouldn't put them off. They'll probably come back with a counter-offer. I'll let you know as soon as I hear from them."

An hour later, Jamie was back on the coastal highway heading to the home of her new client, Brian Greenway. The idea was to meet face-to-face and get an engagement letter signed for their files.

Her first, real client.

Having just made the biggest financial commitment of her life, the timing was perfect.

Jamie plugged the address Colin had given her into her Google Maps app on her phone and almost immediately turned off the coastal highway onto Elk River Road.

Her client's home was at the far end of the road, which followed roughly along the lie of the river to where it curved up against the Grassy Knob Wilderness. Homes were sparse along the back stretch of the road, vying for space in the forest of cedar and tangled vine maples.

When she was about ten minutes from her destination, she tried returning her brother's call, but service was patchy and the call dropped. She'd have to try later, when she was closer to civilization.

The road began to narrow then. She steered through a couple of tight "S" curves, then came to a two story home, built on a hill with a deck built off the upper level. Reflective numbers on a tree beside the driveway assured her this was the right place.

She pulled up beside a black pick-up truck, barely visible behind a screen of hedge cedars.

The air smelt sweet and wild—the way it did at her brother's place. But this home was even farther off the beaten path than Dougal's. And the last stretch of road was a lot steeper and more rugged. She wouldn't want to drive it during a pounding rain storm. That was for sure.

Gripping her briefcase in one hand, she headed for the main door, half expecting a Pit Bull or Rottweiler to come charging at her.

But if her new client owned a dog of any kind, it was an unusually silent breed. As she trod over the pine-needle strewn ground, all she could hear was the sweet song of a nearby chickadee.

The door opened before she reached it, and a man stepped out carrying a leather folder in one hand. He was medium height, slender, with short gray hair and a neatly trimmed beard, also gray. He slipped on a pair of sunglasses, then held out his hand.

"You must be Jamie Lachlan from Howard & Mason."

"I am. Good to meet you Mr. Greenway." His handshake was very firm, and she instinctively tried to see his eyes, only to find her own reflected in the dark blue of his lenses.

"Call me Brian. Hope you don't mind the glasses. I have an extreme sensitivity to sunlight, but it's such a nice day I thought we should conduct our business in the gazebo."

The grass had been clipped in a swath close to the house, and they walked round to the other side where a cedar gazebo sat on a rise of land with a good view of the river. Despite his advanced years, Brian was light on his feet, as spry as a much younger man.

"It's beautiful here."

"Hope you didn't mind the drive."

She gave him a second glance. His voice sounded familiar, but she hadn't as much as spoken to him on the phone yet. It was Colin who had set up the meeting.

"It was fine. I imagine the roads are more challenging in the winter season."

"Wouldn't know. This is my first month here."

"Where did you move from?"

"Oh, I've lived all over. How about you? You sound like you're native to Oregon."

"Born and raised."

"And where'd you go to school?"

She figured he wanted her full credentials, so she gave them to him, adding on her years of experience with Howard & Mason. "I'm looking forward to working with you. Colin says you have an interesting, global portfolio."

"I enjoy investing. And I've had good luck at it. But the tax rules in this country are too much for me."

The gazebo had been screened in and was furnished with a round table and four cushioned chairs. On the table was a bowl filled with ice and several cans of flavored lemonades. Also on the table was a bowl of potato chips and another of roasted peanuts.

"Help yourself to something to drink and to the snacks. I have a summary of my investment portfolio in here"—he indicated the folder he'd been carrying. "Thought I'd show you the sort of stuff I have before we sign that engagement letter of yours."

He had extensive holdings and it took her a while to comprehend the scope of his wealth. She'd been given to understand that Brian Greenway was an eccentric, reclusive millionaire.

The eccentric and reclusive part seemed accurate, but when it came to his wealth, multi-millionaire was more like it.

When their business was concluded, Brian asked if she'd like to walk down to the river.

"Sure."

She followed him, picking her way around large rocks and trees.

"Too bad I'm not a fisherman," Brian said. "Salmon spawn upstream from here in the drainage of Dry Creek."

"Maybe you should take it up."

"Don't think I have the patience. But I sure do love the sound of the water rushing over those stones." Even as he said this, he was jumping from one flat stone to another, working his way closer to the river bank.

"There's a twenty-foot waterfall right here." He held out a hand for her to join him.

Moving much more slowly and cautiously, Jamie followed in his footsteps. It wasn't as easy as it looked since the stones were damp and slick in places.

She wasn't too proud to grab onto Brian's hand when she reached the edge.

"You have to lean over a little," he said, putting a hand to her back for added stability.

She rose on her tip-toes, craned her neck a little further. "I see it! It's gorgeous."

Something underfoot seemed to shift then. Or had Brian let go of her for an instant?

For a split second she was off balance, adrenaline spiking and tingling along her skin.

Then Brian had both hands at her waist, pulling her back to safety. "Careful. These stones are slippery."

Ten minutes later, she was back in her car, glad to be heading for Twisted Cedars. She was approaching the turn onto the coastal highway, when a call came in from Bailey Landax.

The vendors had accepted her offer.

At the end of the month, the house on Horizon Hills Road would be hers.

A moment later, her phone beeped to announce a text message. She waited for the next scenic overlook point, and pulled in to read it. The message was from Wade.

KYLE'S BEEN ARRESTED ON CHARGES OF FRAUD AND CRIMINALLY NEGLIGENT HOMICIDE. THOUGHT YOU SHOULD KNOW.

chapter thirty-four

It was late in the afternoon by the time Dougal and Charlotte were finished giving their statements at the Sheriff's Office. Dougal squeezed Charlotte's hand.

"You okay?"

She nodded. "Hanging in there. Can't wait to get home."

"Mind if I delay you a little longer?" Wade came up from a corridor to their left, indicating they should follow him to his office. "We've found out a few things. I think you both to deserve to know."

Wade waited for them to sit down, before he took his own chair behind his desk.

"Dougal," he said, "Your theory is correct. Joelle Caruthers was indeed Ed Lachlan's daughter. She grew up in foster care after her mother died, and as soon as she turned eighteen legally changed both her first and last names. If I had to guess her motives, she probably wanted to make it hard for her father to ever find her or get in touch."

"Makes perfect sense to me," Dougal said.

"There's more," Wade said. "In the Trash folder on Joelle's email account we found a message from a Hotmail account under the name of Librarianmomma—isn't that the same account that supplied you with those tips about the librarian murders?"

Dougal was on the edge of his seat now. "Yes."

"The message seemed innocuous enough. He just asked how she was doing and did she enjoy being a mother. And it was signed, Dad."

Dougal swore.

"The next day," Wade continued, "Joelle registered for a self-defense class."

"So are you crossing the husband off the suspect list?"

"Pretty much. Seems he took my advice and drove straight home after our encounter at the Linger Longer last night. Video taken when he filled his car with gas at Ashland provides him with an alibi for the medical examiner's estimated time of Joelle's death."

"You guys have had a busy day," Charlotte murmured.

"That's for sure. And Dougal's crazy theory isn't sounding quite so crazy anymore," Wade admitted. "We've got a nation-wide APB out for Ed Lachlan—or whatever he's calling himself these days."

"I hope you find him soon," Dougal said. "I can't help thinking that the only reason he killed Joelle and her baby was to give me a message. And if he somehow finds out, or already knows about Jamie, he could try to hurt her, too."

"I don't follow. What message is he trying to send you?"

Dougal let out a long breath, then glanced at Charlotte, counting on her mere presence beside him to give him strength.

She took his hand. Squeezed it hard.

Then she turned to Wade. "Ed Lachlan wants Dougal to write a book about him. Make him famous."

"You're not suggesting that's why he killed Joelle and her baby?" Wade turned disbelieving eyes to Dougal.

Dougal just shrugged. He knew it sounded outrageous.

But there it was.

* * *

Dougal drove Charlotte from the Sheriff's Office to the market. They hadn't eaten all day, and while neither one had much of an appetite, maybe they would later. Next they picked up Borden, at which point Charlotte offered to take over behind the wheel.

"You still haven't checked in with your sister," she reminded him.

"Thanks." As soon as he was in the passenger seat, Dougal pulled out his phone and tried his sister again. This time, she answered.

"Hey there. I'm parked on a scenic overview on the highway, just a few miles from town."

Dougal turned to Charlotte. "Did you hear that?"

She nodded.

"We're on our way to the cottage. We'll be coming up to you any second. Wait for us."

Five minutes later, they spotted his sister's Miata and Charlotte pulled their vehicle in beside it.

The day was still bright, the sun was hours from setting. Jamie was standing at the guardrail, looking out at the view of the sea stacks. She looked so vulnerable to Dougal in that moment. And precious too.

He left the car and, against all precedent, gave his sister a hug.

"Wow. What was that for?"

"It's been a bad day."

With Charlotte standing by his side, Dougal filled his sister in on everything that had happened. Joelle's murder. The link to their father. And Dougal's interpretation of what it all meant.

Jamie's face turned whiter and whiter.

Charlotte put an arm around her. "It's going to take some time to sink in."

Jamie nodded, mutely.

"So here is the important point, Jamie," Dougal finished. "Our father is here, somewhere around Twisted Cedars. And he could have his sights set on you next. I need you to promise to be careful."

"Our half-sister has just died, and you're worried about me?"

"Of course I am."

"Our father doesn't even know about me, remember? When Mom kicked him out, she didn't tell him she was pregnant."

"Over the years, he may have found out about you. We have the same last name. A simple online directory search would tell him everything he needed to know."

She was quiet for a long time. Then she said. "I met this new client today. He was an elderly man, very wealthy. I did find him a little odd. But he was perfectly harmless. In fact, he led me to this lookout point on the river where he lives to show me a waterfall. If he'd wanted to kill me, all he'd have had to do was give me a shove. Instead, he put out a hand to steady me."

A terrible fear gripped hold of Dougal's heart. "That could have been him. What's his name and address? I'll go check him out."

"Oh, Dougal. I told you. He's harmless. Besides, client information is confidential."

"Will you at least promise not to meet him again, unless you're someplace public? Preferably with me close to hand?"

"Yes, to the first part. Definitely not to the last bit."

"Why do you always make it so difficult for me to look out for you?"

"I promised I'll be careful. And I will."

* * *

Dougal finally felt he could relax when they reached the Librarian Cottage. He and Charlotte cooked dinner together. Shared a bottle of wine. Made love, then stayed up late reading in bed.

Finally, around midnight, Charlotte fell asleep. Her favorite book, *Pride and Prejudice*, had fallen on her chest.

Gently he removed the book, then kissed the tip of her nose.

He was glad she had managed to drift into sleep. He knew he wouldn't.

He got out of bed, put on his clothes, then turned out their bedside lamps. Borden, sleeping on Charlotte's legs, didn't even raise her head.

In the kitchen he thought about pouring himself a glass of scotch.

It was very tempting. But there were dangers on that road, and he figured he'd better avoid them.

If he had stayed in New York, would Joelle and her baby girl still be alive?

He thought, yes.

Wade and Jamie didn't believe it, and Dougal suspected even Charlotte wasn't sure. But he, himself, had no doubt. Ed had killed Joelle and her baby to send him a brutal message.

And if he didn't heed the warning, Jamie could be next.

Dougal settled on the sofa with his laptop. They'd left the windows open and pine-scented air wafted in from the west. He could hear a tree branch rubbing gently, back and forth, against the metal roof.

This place had felt like a haven to him from the first time he saw it. But it didn't feel that way anymore. No place would until he faced his demons.

He opened his email, then composed a new message.

"You win. I'll start the book tomorrow."

Less than a minute after the message was sent, he got his reply from Librarianmomma.

"That's my boy. I can't wait to begin."

THE END

Twisted Cedar Mysteries

buried (Book 1)
forgotten (Book 2)
exposed (Book 3)

* * *

exposed

(Twisted Cedar Mysteries book 3)

When a young boy goes missing shortly after his father is arrested for murdering the boy's mother, the residents of Twisted Cedars are in a panic. They would be even more fearful if they knew a serial murderer has secretly moved back to town. Local Sheriff Wade MacKay, and true crime writer Dougal Lachlan, finally realize that unless they pool their resources and work together, no one in town is going to be safe.

Order your copy of *exposed* (Twisted Cedar Mysteries book 3) now

Excerpt from exposed:

chapter one

Charlotte Hammond had been legal guardian of her dead sister's children, nine-year-old twins Chester and Cory Quinpool, for less than two months when she lost one.

It happened in September, the first week of the new school term. The twins had started fourth grade, time was marching on, they'd be turning ten this November.

No doubt the past year would be one they'd happily put behind them. Only that summer they'd found out their mentally disturbed mother—Charlotte's sister Daisy—hadn't deserted them as originally thought but instead had been killed and illegally buried near an old family cottage.

Less than a month after that shocker, their father, Kyle Quinpool, had been arrested on charges of fraud and criminally negligent homicide. Rather than put his children through the stress of a trial—or so he'd claimed—he'd chosen to plead guilty and serve his sentence.

So...it had been a tough summer.

And now Chester had gone missing somewhere between school and the babysitter's house. The disappearance—which was going to turn into a parent and legal guardian's worst nightmare—began with only a mildly concerning phone call from Nola Thompson, the woman who was supposed to be minding the twins for the hour-and-a-half between school and the closing of the public library where Charlotte worked.

"All the kids have been home for fifteen minutes," Nola said without preamble. "Still no sign of Chester."

He'd ridden his bike today, so if anything, he should have made it to the Thompson house first. "Does Cory know where he is?"

"Nope. Anyway, if he made plans to go to one of his friend's houses, I'm the one who needs to be told. I have enough on my hands without worrying about him." Nola sounded more annoyed than worried.

"He didn't say anything about his plans, either," Charlotte admitted, getting up from her desk and moving down the Mystery aisle so Zoey, shelving books just a few feet from Charlotte's desk, wouldn't hear.

Zoey made a perfectly fine librarian assistant, but since Charlotte had taken custody of the twins, the married mother of three made a point of second-guessing every parenting decision Charlotte made. Given her experience, Zoey probably felt entitled. But Charlotte had seen Zoey with her children, and her hardline approach was not one Charlotte wanted to emulate.

"He's getting to be a real handful," Nola continued, and Charlotte knew it was true.

Earlier that summer she'd sent the kids back to summer camp so they could avoid the local gossip about their parents. But now that school was in session, she couldn't protect them anymore. Cory reacted to the teasing and bullying by being super sweet and accommodating—as if she had to apologize and atone for every one of her parents' sins.

Chester, on the other hand, retaliated with his fists.

Complicating the situation, Charlotte suspected Nola's oldest child, Bruce, was the worst bully of all, so he and Chester were always at odds.

"I'll go looking for him," Charlotte said. "Meanwhile if he does show up please call me right away."

"Fine. But this is the last straw. I'm not going to be able to provide after school care for Chester anymore. Cory, yes. She's an angel. But that brother of hers..."

"Got it." If she sounded short, Charlotte didn't care. It was past time she made alternate arrangements for the twins. Nola Thompson had never been intended to be more than a stop gap solution.

Charlotte grabbed her purse from the bottom drawer of her desk, aware of Zoey hovering nearby.

"I have to leave early. Do you mind locking up?" Charlotte hated to ask the favor, as she knew Zoey would take this as yet another sign of her parental incompetency.

"Sure. Is it Chester, again? If you ask me, that boy is going to turn out just like his father unless you take a firm hand with him."

Charlotte didn't answer, just made her way outside.

She didn't believe Zoey had the answer for how to deal with Chester. But neither did she. Single and twenty-eight-years-old, Charlotte was learning how to parent on the fly.

If the twins had been younger, she might have been more equipped. She had no trouble connecting with the three and four-year-olds who attended her preschool reading circle every week.

But she had less experience with older children. Her boyfriend, true-crime writer Dougal Lachlan, was even more hopeless.

Not that she'd seen much of him lately. Since the twins had moved in, he'd become increasingly reclusive. Given the issues he had with his own father, she guessed he wasn't keen on stepping into any sort of parental role himself.

Or maybe he was just getting tired of her.

Outside Charlotte slipped on her sunglasses. September was often one of the nicest weather months for coastal Oregon and today was a perfect example. Sunny, hot, almost no wind. Since she lived only a few blocks from the library she never drove to work, which meant she had to walk home to get her car. She hurried along Ocean Way pathway, barely smiling as she crossed paths with the mother of one of her favorite teenaged patrons.

When she reached the gracious Victorian home where she'd grown up, her first instinct was to check the garage for Chester's bike. It wasn't there. She went through the mudroom into the house.

"Chester? Are you home?" She ran through the entire house, checking every room, including the bedroom that had once been Daisy's and was now the twins'. She suspected Chester had agreed to share the room with his sister, because he knew she was afraid to be alone.

What would Cory do if they didn't find her brother? If he——?

No. She couldn't let herself think that way.

Next Charlotte checked the yard, and then the beach that stretched out on either side of her property. No luck in either place.

The school was the next logical place to go.

Her car, which she kept in the garage on the side of her generous ocean front lot, was a '97 BMW convertible that had belonged to her father. The BMW hardly fit her librarian image. A lot of people were surprised she'd kept the vehicle after her parents' death several years ago. But every time she settled into the low-slung seat and started the engine, Charlotte felt a secret thrill.

She was not one for adventures. She hated travel, was deathly afraid of public speaking and generally chose the safest and most practical course in any situation. Driving this car was her one indulgence.

Not counting her affair with Dougal, who'd moved back to Twisted Cedars from New York City just that spring. A bestselling author now, he'd grown up on the poor side of town, drawn to trouble and rebellion from an early age. He'd grown into a brooding, somewhat enigmatic man, with dark Irish good looks—though he was from Scottish stock on his father's side—and a talent for investigating old crimes and getting to the heart of the matter.

She still couldn't quite believe that he was not only attracted to her, but that he actually seemed to like her. A lot.

Or at least he had. Before she'd become an instant guardian to two nine-year-olds.

Charlotte backed out of the driveway, shifted gears, then hit the gas a little too hard, throwing up bits of gravel and causing her body to lurch forward, then abruptly back. She gripped the steering wheel like it was a throw line and she was a drowning swimmer, and pushed her speed beyond the town limit.

In less than thirty seconds she was at the park. The

manicured green space led to a public beach on the other side of the sand dunes. Closer to the main road, screened off from the danger of traffic and ocean by shrubbery and a chain-link fence, was a playground. The children clambering on the monkey bars and swings were all much younger than Chester, but Charlotte approached one of the mothers sitting on a nearby bench, scrolling on her mobile phone.

"Hi! I'm looking for my nephew. He's nine-years-old, sandy-colored hair and wearing a dark green T-shirt and jeans. Have you seen anyone like that?"

The woman, who was cute and looked twenty, if that, gave her a blank stare. Then she shook her head. "Sorry. I haven't."

"Right. Thanks anyway." Charlotte dashed to the dunes, and the beach beyond. Though going near the ocean without adult supervision was strictly forbidden, at this point she would have been relieved to spot him on the expansive sandy shoreline.

Quickly she scanned the scattering of people out enjoying the beautiful day. No children close to Chester's age here either.

Now she'd go to the school, and hope that at least one of the teachers was still around.

Charlotte's pulse was a loud, steady tattoo in her ear drums as she got out of the car, cell phone in one hand, keys in the other. She found the main doors locked. Now what?

According to her watch, school had been out of session for fifty minutes now. She left the paved sidewalk and jogged across the freshly mown lawn that ran down the side of the one-story brick structure, hoping for an open window and someone nearby to hear her call out.

Within seconds she heard the faint sound of a woman speaking, her tone lecturing, though no words were distinguishable. Charlotte traced the sound to an open window, which she guessed—having spent a lot of time in the school the past two weeks—was the staff room.

"Hello!" She was tall, and had no trouble looking in the

window. About eight women, and a couple men, were seated throughout a room furnished with two round tables, a sofa and several arm chairs. "I'm sorry to interrupt but my nephew Chester Quinpool didn't come home from school today."

As she spoke, she focused one by one on the teachers' faces. Most were familiar to her. The school lacked funding for a proper library and so often made use of the public one which was, after all, only a ten minute walk away.

"Charlotte?" Olivia Young, the twins' teacher, came to the window. "Weren't Cory and Chester supposed to go to the Thompsons' after school today?"

Olivia was in her early thirties, newly married, and if Charlotte wasn't mistaken, newly pregnant, as well. They'd had several meetings already to discuss the twins and how to best help them transition into the new school year.

Charlotte liked certain things about Olivia. She had a calm, gentle manner about her, and seemed genuinely concerned about the twins and sensitive to the problems they might have as they adjusted to their new reality. But a few times she'd displayed flashes of salacious curiosity, obviously hoping Charlotte would fill in some of the gaps, provide the "inside story" on what had really happened to Daisy all those years ago.

Her curiosity was understandable, in a way. Daisy's death, her secret burial, and Kyle's cover-up was undeniably the most dramatic event that had taken place in Twisted Cedars for the past decade.

Actually, no. There had been another tragedy in Twisted Cedars this summer, one involving a young wife from Ashland and her baby daughter. But no one in town had known that family, whereas Daisy and Kyle were the sort of people everyone knew about.

"Yes," Charlotte responded, in answer to Olivia's question. "And Cory did go, but Chester did not. I was—" She let out a deep breath of disappointment. "Hoping maybe you'd kept him after class."

Olivia's green eyes widened. "Oh, in that case I would

have called you. Immediately."

Yes. She'd been afraid of that.

"Why don't you come inside, Charlotte? I'll go unlock the door."

It was the principal speaking now, Gabrielle Hodges, an athletic, somewhat masculine looking woman in her late fifties. She'd been the fourth grade teacher back when Charlotte was a student.

"I have to keep looking for Chester."

"We'll do a full search here," Gabrielle assured her, "Just to make sure he isn't hiding anywhere."

"Thank you." Charlotte's glanced back at Ashley. "Can you think of any incident that came up today, something involving Chester, that might help explain where he's gone?"

Ashley's brow furrowed as she rubbed the side of her face. "He seemed...troubled. But that's not unusual."

No, sadly, it was not.

"I don't want to alarm you," Gabrielle said. "He's probably gone to a friend's house or something. But I'm going to call 911."

Adrenaline buzzed through Charlotte's system and her stomach tightened like she'd been sucker punched. Alerting the authorities elevated the situation and possibilities that had seemed remote at first, possibilities like abduction or worse, could no longer be pushed to the back of her mind.

For what felt like the hundredth time she glanced at her watch. Chester had now been missing for almost one hour.

"Yes. Call 911."

"And I'll get out my class list and phone all the parents," Olivia offered.

"Thank you." There was hardly anyone left in the staff room now, as teachers fanned out to search for the missing boy, and Gabrielle and Olivia went to make their calls.

Charlotte jogged back to the sidewalk, trying to decide what to do next.

Though it was a possibility that had to be crossed off the list, she didn't think they'd find Chester hiding on school property. She supposed she could drive up and down the main streets of town in the hopes of spotting him or his bike.

Then inspiration struck. Maybe Chester had gone to see his grandfather, Jim Quinpool. For a few years—before they divorced and Muriel moved away—Kyle's parents had lived with him and the twins. If Chester was upset, his grandfather was an obvious person to run to.

As she hurried back to her car, she called Jim. The phone rang and rang on the other end, but there was no answer. That didn't mean Jim wasn't home. He'd wanted custody of the twins after his son went to prison, and he'd been ticked off when the court appointed her, instead. Possibly he'd seen her name on call display and refused to answer out of spite.

So she'd just have to go flush him out. On the drive to Jim's place—he now lived in an apartment above the realtor business he'd once run with Kyle—she tried Wade McKay, the Curry County Sheriff and a personal friend.

The 911 call would be routed through his office. But she wanted to speak to him personally.

Wade answered after the first ring.

"Charlotte. We just got the call from Gabrielle Hodges. Where are you?"

"In my car, on my way to J-Jim's place." She swallowed. At the first sound of Wade's voice, she'd had a sudden urge to cry.

But she couldn't break down now. She had to be strong and hope for the best. That she would find Chester soon and he'd be fine.

"I've already checked the Twisted Cedars Park and the beach. Chester's teacher is calling everyone in his class and the rest of the staff are searching the school."

"That's good. Drive carefully Charlotte. Try to stay calm. I'm sending out every available vehicle to comb this town. Chances are good we'll find him in the next half an hour or so."

"He rode his bike to school today, Wade. He could—he might be miles away by now."

"A boy on his bike outside of town limits is sure to attract notice. We'll find him Charlotte."

Even as he said that, Charlotte passed a black and white SUV with "Sheriff Curry County" stenciled on the side panel. The driver, Deputy Dunne, gave her a wave and a nod, as if to say, "Don't worry ma'am. We're on this."

Before Dougal moved back to Twisted Cedars, she and Wade had dated. He'd even asked her to marry him once—though she was pretty sure he hadn't loved her at the time. For sure he didn't love her now. But she was grateful he wasn't the sort of man to hold a grudge.

"Thanks Wade. I just—Thank you."

"Of course. Keep in touch. Let me know what happens at Jim's."

Charlotte ended the call, but kept a tight hold on her phone. Please ring. Please be Nola, saying Chester had finally shown up. Or Olivia, saying Chester was fine, he'd gone home with a school friend...

But her phone remained silent.

She wished desperately that she had a way to reach Chester directly. The twins owned iPads which they weren't allowed to bring to school. But they didn't have phones. Their father had said they had to wait until they turned thirteen—a rule that had seemed reasonable to Charlotte, once.

Now she swore that as soon as they found Chester, she would go out and get them, not just phones, but possibly GPS tracking devises she'd strap to their ankles.

Charlotte turned onto Driftwood Lane, the town's main drag, grateful that August was over and there was plenty of available parking. She was able to pull into a space right outside Quinpool Realty. The business was closed. It had been since Kyle's arrest.

She rushed out of her car, glancing around, hoping to see, if not Chester, then at least his bike. But neither one was in sight. Maybe he'd locked his bike up in the back. She opened the door to the left of the glass door to Quinpool Realty, and then climbed up a narrow, steep flight of stairs to the upper apartment.

With each step her heart seemed to thump harder. Sweat rose on her hands, filming slickly against the phone and keys she was carrying. She put both into her pockets, then rubbed her palms on the light wool blend of her skirt.

At the top of the stairs was a small landing and a wooden door with a peep hole and a slot for mail. She listened, straining for the sound of Chester's voice within, but all she could hear was the faint drone of a television.

She rapped on the door, waiting less than ten seconds before repeating.

"Jim?" she called out. "It's Charlotte. I'm looking for Chester."

Finally he opened. Behind him was a dimly lit room with a sofa and television. The room had a foul, stale, alcoholic odor. And so did Jim.

He looked rough. Unshaven, clothes rumpled as if he'd slept in them—for more than one night, hair that had gone too long without a wash, or a cut. Considering he'd once been one of the better dressed men in town, it was a long fall.

The man obviously needed help, but she couldn't worry about that right now.

"Is Chester here?" She scanned the room as she asked this. When she tried to step forward, Jim blocked her.

"No, he isn't. What the hell is going on?"

Charlotte stared at him, not knowing what to say. She would have given anything to see her nephew sitting on that disgusting couch, eating junk food and watching sit-com reruns with his grandfather.

But he wasn't here.

He wasn't at Nola's, or at home, or the school or the park or any of the normal places he liked to hang out.

So where was he?

Charlotte's mind went blank as a terrible fear took grip of her body and soul.

Dougal had warned her that the horror that had gripped their town the past few months wasn't over. Kyle Quinpool may have been arrested. Her sister's death was being avenged. But there was a bigger evil lurking in Twisted Cedars.

She didn't want to believe it. But it seemed there was a very good chance Chester's disappearance was linked to that.

End of excerpt – We hope you enjoyed it.

note from the author

I'd like to thank the people who helped me with this novel, my editor Linda Style, formatter Meredith Bond, proofreader Toni Hyatt, and cover designer Frauke Spanuth from CrocoDesigns.

For help with my research, I am indebted to Deputy George Simpson, as well as friends Sue and Greg McCormick who introduced me to the Deputy, as well as shared impressions and memories of their years living in Oregon. Thank you also to District Attorney Everett Dial who patiently answered many questions from me over the phone.

I'm very grateful to the friends and family members who have read preliminary copies of my Twisted Cedars Mysteries and provided much needed feedback: Mike Fitzpatrick, Kathy Eliuk, Voula Cocolakis, Lorelle Binnion, Susan Lee, Brenda Collins, Donna Tunney, Gloria Fournier, Sue McCormick and Greg McCormick...thank you all!

about the author

C.J. Carmichael has published over 40 novels and has twice been nominated for a RITA award from the Romance Writers of America. CJ likes to write stories about mystery, romance, small communities and intrigue. She's inspired by real-life scenarios...the kind you read about in magazines and watch on the nightly news on television. When it's time to take a break from the computer, she heads to the Rocky Mountains near her home in Calgary where she lives with her partner Michael. She's especially proud of her two best masterpieces—Lorelle and Tessa, her daughters. If you'd like to learn more about her books, check out her website: http://cjcarmichael.com and please do sign up for her newsletter.

other novels by C.J. Carmichael

Carrigans of the Circle C (western drama and romance)
Promise Me, Cowboy (story 1)
Good Together (story 2)
Close To Her Heart (story 3)
Snowbound in Montana (story 4)
A Cowgirl's Christmas (story 5)

Family Matters (family drama and romance)
A Daughter's Place (story 1)
Her Best Friend's Baby (story 2)
The Fourth Child (story 3)

Twisted Cedars Mysteries
Buried (book 1)
Forgotten (book 2)
Exposed (book 3)

For C. J. Carmichael's complete backlist, please visit her website: http://cjcarmichael.com

CPSIA information can be obtained
at www.ICGtesting.com
Printed in the USA
LVHW04s1539280518
578747LV00013B/1519/P